Moonlit

He drew her into a s _____ bench. In this part of _____ there was no light except for that shed on them by a quarter moon. Suddenly realizing where their steps had carried them, Bella lifted her eyebrows.

"What are you about, Harry?"

He gave her a slow, lazy, decidedly wicked smile that made her toes tingle. "I haven't been able to keep my mind on my painting since that kiss we shared in my studio. Have you thought of it, midget?"

"I am not a midget," Bella fussed, but she sat by him as he wished her to do.

"Have you thought of my kisses, little amazon?"

"That's better!"

"Bella!" His voice was a low, urgent growl.

"I have, much good it will do either of us."

He slid his arm around her shoulders, urging her closer to him. "Nonsense, for it tells us that we must repeat the experience."

She shook her head, but the sight of his light eyes glittering in the moonlight was doing strange things to her breathing. . . .

Isabella's Rake

by

June Calvin

A SIGNET BOOK

SIGNET
Published by the Penguin Group
Penguin Books USA Inc., 375 Hudson Street,
New York, New York 10014, U.S.A.
Penguin Books, Ltd, 27 Wrights Lane,
London W8 5TZ, England
Penguin Books Australia Ltd, Ringwood,
Victoria, Australia
Penguin Books Canada Ltd, 10 Alcorn Avenue,
Toronto, Ontario, Canada M4V 3B2
Penguin Books (N.Z.) Ltd, 182–190 Wairau Road,
Auckland 10, New Zealand

Penguin Books Ltd, Registered Offices:
Harmondsworth, Middlesex, England

First published by Signet, an imprint of Dutton Signet,
a division of Penguin Books USA Inc.

First Printing, June, 1997
10 9 8 7 6 5 4 3 2 1

 REGISTERED TRADEMARK—MARCA REGISTRADA

Printed in the United States of America

BOOKS ARE AVAILABLE AT QUANTITY DISCOUNTS WHEN USED TO PROMOTE PRODUCTS OR
SERVICES. FOR INFORMATION PLEASE WRITE TO PREMIUM MARKETING DIVISION, PENGUIN
BOOKS USA INC., 375 HUDSON STREET, NEW YORK, NEW YORK 10014.

To Hilary Ross, with thanks not only for buying and editing my books but also for caring deeply about the Regency genre. Readers as well as writers of our genre owe her a debt of gratitude.

Chapter One

"Hurry! Before someone sees us!" Blond curls bouncing, Isabella Eardley motioned her friend to follow her as she clattered down the servants' stairs.

Virginia Douglas protested as she followed Isabella, "They're sure to hear us. We sound like a herd of horses going down these wooden stairs."

Isabella halted abruptly, causing Virginia to slam into her. "You're right. Tiptoe!" Slowly, silently the two conspirators made their way to the bottom, smothering their giggles. Isabella stuck her head cautiously around the door frame to survey the hall. "Shhh. Mustn't let the housekeeper hear us. Mrs. Plimpton would tell on us for sure."

Isabella looked down the hall in the direction of the housekeeper's quarters, and then in the other direction, toward the kitchen. "Now!"

Quickly, their slippers making swishing noises on the polished wooden floor, the two girls hastened to the kitchen. Then, with calm dignity, Isabella pushed on the swinging door and entered the room.

"Miss Bella! Never say the card party is over already?"

"No, Mrs. Filmore. But my friend here—oh! May I present Miss Virginia Douglas? Ginny, this is our esteemed day-cook, Mrs. Filmore."

Virginia curtsied quickly, causing the rotund cook to flush deeply as she sank into a curtsey of her own. "Why, miss, t'aint for you to bend the knee to the likes of me!" But Virginia could tell that Mrs. Filmore was pleased by her gesture of respect.

"We came because Grandmama's guests ate up all of your poppyseed cakes before Virginia could get one, and after I had been bragging that they were the best in all of England."

Mrs. Filmore fluttered excitedly at this extravagant compliment. "She shall have some, then. Fair lucky it is that I set some aside for the upper servants' tea. But they shall have lemon cake and never be the wiser." She motioned to a kitchen maid who had been observing all of this while drying pots and pans. "Quick, girl. Fetch that tray of poppyseed cakes from the larder."

"May we have some lemonade to wash them down with? And then I think perhaps you should send something more upstairs for our guests, for Grandmama would be vexed if we were to run short." Isabella looked expectantly at the cook.

"Oh, yes indeed, though why Mr. Hilliard hasn't sent a footman down to fetch something, I'm sure I don't know!"

Isabella winked at Virginia, who was already making suitably appreciative noises over the confection she was nibbling. The two girls munched cakes and sipped lemonade while Mrs. Filmore disappeared into the larder and emerged with a giant tray laden with baked goods.

"I'd best take this up meself. Bridey would drop it, sure."

Bridey scowled at this. As soon as Mrs. Filmore had disappeared, Isabella jumped up. "Here, girl. Finish what we've left, won't you? I'm full, but Mrs. Filmore would be offended if I left anything." She pushed the plate bearing the last two seed cakes toward the thin young servant.

"Oh, may I, miss?" Bridey didn't wait for the invitation to be repeated, but grabbed up the cakes. "I'd best get out of sight to eat 'em, though." She darted into the larder.

Left alone, the two girls exchanged conspiratorial glances. "Shall we take a walk?" Bella's bright blue eyes fairly crackled with excitement.

"All by ourselves?" Virginia's eyes widened at the daring proposal. Bella held her breath during the brief but suspenseful hesitation. Then Virginia nodded eagerly. "Yes, let's!"

"Famous!" Isabella grabbed Virginia's hand, and they made their escape out the kitchen door. The steps led down to an alley perpendicular to Grosvenor Square. Isabella turned the other way, heading for the mews.

"We'll go over to Brook Street for a stroll," she said, grinning at her companion.

"Won't your grooms stop you?"

"Mitchell might, he's the head groom. But he should be having his tea and gin about now."

As she had predicted, the other stable workers did little more than glance at the two young girls, and in short order they were walking along tree-lined Brook Street.

"Isn't it wonderful to be out of that stuffy drawing room! Where shall we go?" Skipping for joy at her freedom, Isabella twirled around in front of Virginia, her blue-sprigged white muslin dress molding to her legs as she moved.

"Oh, I . . ."

"Let's go to Somerset House and look at the paintings."

Virginia frowned. "Isn't that several blocks from here?"

"I've walked it many times." Isabella cast her partner in crime a disdainful look.

Virginia's chin came up. "It isn't that I can't walk that far. I'm a country girl, after all. But I've no parasol, and my skin would burn to a crisp."

Isabella scowled up at the sun. "You are right; so would I, and then Grandmother would know I've left the house unattended."

Isabella looked closely at the beautiful girl in front of her. Her red-gold hair shimmered in the sun, and her fair skin was touched with the same delicate color and perfect smoothness of a peach. "You don't have freckles, which is unusual with hair that color."

"I've worked very hard to get rid of them, always avoiding the sun and using so many preparations, sometimes I thought my skin would fall off from it all!"

Isabella giggled. "I turn a nice gold color in the sun, but Mama and Papa are scandalized because I like it. They declare I look like a farm hand when I tan. We shall stay in the shade and have a comfortable coze for a while, then slip back in before the party ends."

Relieved, her new friend linked her arm with Bella's and smiled. "Aren't these card parties the most boring thing ever invented?"

"Especially when Grandmama's friends take it so seriously. Mrs. Gardenhire looked like she was going to eat her partner alive when she trumped her suit! It is so wonderful to find someone my own age. I never thought London could be so dull as it has since the poor mad king died in January."

Virginia nodded. "Mama says it will not be a gay season, at least not until the six months are up."

The two girls seated themselves on a bench under a tree and silently enjoyed the pleasures of a warm April day for a few minutes.

"You are fond of visiting the gallery at Somerset House?" Virginia inquired politely.

Isabella's demeanor changed. All hints of levity or languor disappeared. "Yes, for I am an artist, you see. A professional artist!" She gestured expansively. "I want to paint grand landscapes. I mean to be England's first great female landscape artist."

Virginia was startled and impressed by her new friend's ambition. Seriousness of purpose gave to the petite young woman an unexpected air of maturity. "I did not know a female could hope for such an accomplishment," she said, admiration in her voice.

"It is going to be very difficult. I wanted to enroll in the Royal Academy, but they wouldn't let me because I am female. Did you ever hear of anything so unreasonable!"

Virginia made sympathetic noises. "Parents are so very unreasonable about everything."

"My father is, at least, but I am not speaking of him, but of the Academy itself. It doesn't accept female pupils, which is of all things ridiculous, for was not Angelica Kaufman a founding member?"

"Oh!" Virginia's full peach lips pulled down in sympathy. "It is too bad of them. But can't you hire a private teacher?"

"Grandmama hired Mr. Morgan to teach me, but he thinks ladies should learn only to sketch and do watercolors. He has finally condescended to teach me how to do miniatures in oil, but I want to paint real paintings. Big canvases!" Isabella gestured widely with her hands. "And I want to take the life classes at the Academy."

"You will think me very ignorant, but what . . . ?"

"That's where you draw from living models. Men and women pose for you."

Virginia's eyes widened. "Without clothes?" At Bella's nod, she shook her head. "No wonder they won't let you!"

"If only I were a boy!" Bella sighed.

"Perhaps you could dress as one." Virginia looked eagerly at Isabella. "Once when I was not yet out of the schoolroom, my cousin Gil loaned me his inexpressibles so I could go with him to a cock fight."

"I tried that once, but I was recognized immediately by Lord Dudley. He said I looked like a pouter pigeon." Isabella glanced ruefully at her chest.

Virginia studied her friend's ample endowment and giggled. "Yes, I can see the problem. Obviously not one from which I suffer!" She gestured at her own small, high bosom, enhanced by cleverly arranged frills. "I envy you a little! How shall I attract a truly exciting man when gentlemen set so much store by a woman's figure?"

Isabella flounced on the bench. "Well, don't envy me! It is a great bother, having men ogle me so. Not just young, attractive gentlemen, but old men, too! I wish to paint, not attract men. But my grandmother says I *must* marry. She says a woman cannot remain single, so when the season finally begins, the art lessons will cease, and all my time will be spent looking for a titled husband!"

Virginia cried out dramatically, "I, too, am being urged to marry, though my family has had my groom selected ever since I was born! He has a title and is my second cousin, and that is quite enough for them. Never mind that he has hair the color of carrots and more freckles than any hound, and is as dull and proper as a stick."

"You are speaking of Lord Threlbourne, are you not? Is he the one who loaned you his inexpressibles?"

Virginia's mouth drew into a mulish line. "Yes. But that was when we were young. He is always lecturing about propriety now. They kept me home last year when I should have had my come-out, because I told them I wouldn't marry him. And I won't! I won't be forced to marry him!"

"No, that would be odious, though he seems very nice."

"Nice! Nice!" Virginia clenched her hands. "That is just it. He is insipid. So gentle and polite and . . . and sweet! There is not a jot of the romantical about him, and besides, if we married, all of our children would be sure to be freckled, with him for the father and me for the mother!"

Isabella commiserated with her. "I find freckles delightful, but it is true that they are far from fashionable. It is not so bad for a man such as Lord Threlbourne, but for a woman, I can see that it would be a sore trial."

"You do understand! All of the lemon juice I have had to endure. And oatmeal packs and ointments and nostrums. I will not visit it upon my daughters if I can help it."

"Well, I shall help you to find a gentleman with fashionably pale skin. My grandmother knows every titled family in the peerage. I am sure she can find someone for you."

"He would have to be very highly placed, and wealthy

too, to make my parents give up trying to wed me to Gilbert."

"Still, we shall manage it."

Isabella's determination gave her friend courage. "And *I* shall help *you*, somehow. Perhaps after the season begins, I can hire an artist and you can come to my house for lessons."

"Would your parents . . . ?"

"My mama would dearly love to see me cultivate some feminine accomplishments. She finds my love of horses and fly-fishing to be entirely inappropriate in a young lady."

"Hmmmm. But I do not think they could hire Mr. Maillot. He is the one I wish to teach me."

"Who is Mr. Maillot?" Virginia asked.

"He is an advanced student at the Academy. Everyone says he will be the next Turner."

At Virginia's blank look, Isabella explained. "J. M. W. Turner, the most famous landscape artist in England."

"Oh. I see you must take me in hand and educate me."

"When Grandmama was inquiring about art instruction for me, she learned about him. He is said to be quite a good teacher. But he refused her request that he come to our house to give me lessons. He doesn't take female pupils, you see. I do wish I could disguise myself as a man, but Eden—she was my governess—says it is quite impossible."

Virginia studied her new friend gravely. "Let me look at you. Stand up and turn around," she commanded. Pleased to be taken so seriously, Isabella turned silently while Virginia surveyed her from head to toe.

"No, you are too short, and far too pretty to be disguised as a man, even if it were not for your bosom."

Depressed, Isabella slumped back down on the bench.

"But . . ." Virginia cocked her head thoughtfully.

"What?"

"You *could* pass for a boy."

"A boy!"

"Yes. My mother has a page who is every bit as pretty as you. His lips are even full like yours." Virginia hesitated, afraid she had insulted her new friend by alluding to this undesirable trait. When she saw that Bella was attending her eagerly, she continued. "He's about your height—a chubby fellow of nine or ten, and his head is all over blond ringlets. Momma loves to have him follow her about to carry her packages and open doors for her. She rescued him from a chimney sweep four years ago, and plans to make a footman of him when he is older. She has other pages, too. She is always rescuing people, you see."

"Oh, how lovely! All of my relatives are much too self-involved to be so kind."

"You could borrow some of his clothes. I daresay the ruffles on his shirt would help disguise your . . . you know."

"Ruffles? On a servant's shirt?"

"Yes. Mama thinks it quite droll to dress him in ruffles, lace, and knee britches, something like an eighteenth-century gentleman, though without the powdered wig."

Would it work? Isabella's heart pounded with excitement. "I want to see him. Let's go to your house at once."

Virginia giggled. "He is sitting in your front hall right now, waiting until the end of the party so he can accompany us home."

Isabella stood abruptly. "Let's go. We must get back before the end of the party anyway, or we shall be in the suds."

Virginia fairly trotted to keep up with Isabella, though her legs were much longer than the younger girl's. "Wait! How will you manage it? This Mr. Maillot would doubtless wonder about such an unusual costume, for one thing."

Isabella never slowed her pace. "That's easy. You will

go with me. You can pose as your mother. You'll say you have noticed that your page is very talented, and wish to offer him an education. We'll pay whatever he asks. I have pots of money."

"Wouldn't you be missed if you were gone often enough to take lessons?"

"Hmmm. I need to think about that awhile." Bella paused momentarily to ponder the problem.

"I know! We can tell my parents I am visiting you, and your grandmother that you are visiting me!" Virginia fairly bounced with enthusiasm.

"I knew you were a kindred spirit!" Isabella hugged the taller girl before hurrying them both through the mews, past the surprised cook, up the servants' staircase, and into the withdrawing room to which they had repaired before making their escape from the duchess's card party.

The two girls were catching their breath and tucking disordered curls into place when the Dowager Duchess of Carminster entered the room. "Where have you been, Bella? And don't tell me right here, for I sent two different maids to seek you!"

The tall, dignified elderly woman with the iron gray hair and the imperious voice loomed over the young girls in a manner calculated to intimidate. But Bella gave no signs of being intimidated. Instead, an angelic expression on her face, she told her grandmother the truth, at least part of it. "Those marvelous seed cakes of Mrs. Filmore's—I had bragged to Virginia about them, and then they disappeared so fast, she hadn't a chance to try one."

"Never tell me you went to the kitchen yourself! Why did you not send a footman?" The duchess thumped the cane she carried against the floor for emphasis.

"Well, I also wanted to show Virginia my paintings. We went to my studio first, and then we got some cakes for ourselves. Oh! And we stepped outside to eat them, because it was so very hot in the kitchen. You may ask Mrs. Filmore."

"And I shall! Never you doubt it! But whatever were you thinking, eating in the alley? Have a care for your reputation, Bella!"

"Grandmama, no one saw us but a delivery boy."

The duchess began to draw in a deep breath, obviously about to ring a severe peal over her granddaughter's head. Virginia hastened to the rescue. "Isabella is so very talented, Your Grace. I am all over with envy, for in spite of my mama's best efforts, I am sadly lacking in artistic accomplishments."

The duchess exhaled. Her expression softened. Though Isabella constantly exasperated her by her high spirits, she was sufficiently fond of the girl to be susceptible to such praise. "Yes, Mr. Morgan says she is improving vastly under his tutelage. But come, child. Our guests are leaving. You will be accounted a very rude chit indeed if you do not bid them farewell."

Isabella stood. "Excuse me, Grandmama. I quite forgot. Come, Virginia. Let us hurry—"

"No! Slowly. How many times must I tell you a lady moves with dignity and grace?"

The two girls checked momentarily at this reminder, but before they reached the bottom of the stairs had begun half running again, leaving the duchess to mutter to herself, "Lady Douglas told me her gel was a trial to her, and I can see now that they are alike as two peas in a pod."

Chapter Two

"Nothing fits but the boots!" Isabella turned from side to side in front of the mirror in Virginia's bedroom, studying the male garments she was wearing. The ruffled shirt hung on her petite frame. The breeches were too loose in the waist, though they fit snugly in the hips.

Virginia nodded. "I told you he was chubby. But that is all to the good. This way, we can add padding to make you look like a chubby boy, instead of a curvaceous girl. Here, try this." Virginia handed Isabella a bolster pillow.

Tongue sticking out slightly from the left side of her mouth, Isabella tried stuffing the pillow under her bosom inside the ruffled shirt. "It's too much. It won't bend."

"We'll find something. Perhaps some sheets or pillow cases." Virginia ran from the room and returned a few minutes later with an armful of items raided from the linen closet. Silence reigned in the room as the two young girls padded the clothing of Clarence, Mrs. Douglas's page.

"There!" Satisfied with her efforts, Virginia turned Isabella to face the mirror.

Bella grinned at her reflection. "Wonderful! I look just like him."

"Well, not quite. I think you will still have to bind yourself somewhat, but—"

"Oh, Ginny!" Bella gave her friend an exuberant hug. "It's going to work! Now all we have to do is figure out how to elude Grandmama, your mother, and my companion."

Virginia looked a little daunted at this list. "And Gilbert! He has appointed himself my guardian in my father's absence."

"I had hoped perhaps Lord Threlbourne might assist us."

"Merciful heavens, no. Gilbert is all propriety. He would never dream of assisting a young girl in eluding her chaperones!"

"Well, the first thing to do is send Clarence out to purchase another uniform, right down to the boots, for I will want this one too often to borrow it."

"There is a lady below who wishes to speak with you."

Jean Maillot ignored his manservant to continue meticulously applying paint to a large canvas.

"Shall I send her up?"

"Tell her to come back this evening. I'm working."

"No, I mean a real lady. Dressed in the first stare of fashion. With a ridiculous little page to carry her packages."

Maillot turned irritated eyes toward his servant. "Damn! What does such a one want with me? Did you tell her I don't do portraits?"

"Yes, sir. She wishes to see you about art instruction."

"Worse yet. Get rid of her. You know I don't waste my time instructing females. Particularly aristocratic ones."

"I tried. She insisted on speaking to you. Said she would not accept a refusal from a mere servant."

With a growl of fury the short, dark-haired man wiped his hands clean, tore off his smock, and stalked from the room.

He stormed into his parlor, then checked himself. An exceptionally pretty young woman with golden red hair turned toward him. Her walking dress of forest green, with a green striped spencer, brought out the green in her eyes. She held a furled parasol that matched her spencer. She was a vision, and Jean Maillot, like most artists, appreciated beauty wherever he found it.

"Mr. Maillot, I trust?" The vision haughtily interrupted his survey of her person.

"At your service." He bowed politely, then accepted the visiting card she handed him. "Lady Douglas? I am honored by your visit to my most unworthy abode. Won't you have a seat? May I offer you some tea?"

Regally seating herself in the indicated chair, Virginia declined tea. "When I made inquiries at the Royal Academy, you were highly recommended as an instructor in drawing and painting."

Maillot sighed. "I do teach art, madam, but I do not take female pupils, much as I hate to admit it in the presence of such beauty."

She frowned at him. "Why is that, if I may ask?"

Maillot cleared his throat nervously. "Serious art instruction requires a concentration and application that is beyond the female mind."

"I beg to—"

Maillot held up his hand. "Even in that rare female who is intellectually capable, the demands made upon her mental faculties by serious study might be injurious to her health. I would not wish to be responsible for the results."

It appeared that Lady Douglas would argue with him, but the cherubic page by her side, clutching a large portfolio, cleared his throat loudly.

The young woman turned to look at him and then nodded briskly. "I strongly disagree with you, sir, but as I do not seek instruction myself, our difference of opinion need not concern us at this time." Imitating her mother at her grandest, Virginia waved a dismissive hand at the artist.

"Your intended pupil is my page. Step forward, Clarence, and show Mr. Maillot your portfolio."

Isabella opened the portfolio and took out a sheaf of drawings. She held them out to Mr. Maillot, who stared at her without reaching for them.

"*This* is my intended pupil?"

"Clarence is very talented, sir. He—"

"He is a child. What, eight or nine? I fear you have been misinformed, madam. I take only advanced pupils, who are preparing to enter the Royal Academy."

"There is no reason why Clarence could not—"

"I have had some instruction, Mr. Maillot," Isabella declared. "I am far from a rank amateur."

Maillot's eyes narrowed suspiciously upon hearing Isabella's voice. "A very well-spoken page, madam, upon my word! One might almost take him for one of the quality."

"I see that all of my servants learn to speak properly," Virginia declared, trying again for her mother's most impressive voice. "Please be so kind as to look at his drawings."

"Before I look at his work, I wish to have a closer look at *him*!" Maillot grabbed Isabella's elbow and jerked her up close to him. The violence of his movements caused her to drop the handful of drawings. As they hit the bare wood floor, they fanned out and drifted away on the polished surface.

"Sir, I will thank you not to manhandle my page," Virginia objected, beginning to be a little frightened.

Isabella held herself straight and steady, meeting the hostile dark eyes without blinking. "I know I look young, sir, but I am rising twelve and—"

She stifled an indignant gasp as Maillot turned her about roughly to study her from behind.

"'Tis not your youth I object to." He gestured at Isabella's well-rounded derriere. "I'll have you know that I won't—"

"Teach such ridiculously attired persons," drawled a deep masculine voice.

The three turned as one to see who had spoken. A tall man sauntered across the room, several of Isabella's drawings in his hand. He was an exquisite-looking gentleman. His form-fitting brown coat showed the hand of a master tailor, and his pleated buff kerseymere trousers, buttoned under the instep, fit his muscular legs like a second skin. His wavy hair shone like a newly minted guinea, and his pale blue eyes glittered as he surveyed first Virginia, then Isabella.

This is Adonis, come to life, Isabella thought as she studied his profile. *That head could be the model for a Greek coin.* For the first time in her young life a jolt of awareness of herself as a woman startled her as his eyes met hers.

Maillot once again turned Isabella about by her elbow so that her back was to them. "Harry, look at this," he ordered, gesturing to the rounded bottom. You know as well as I—"

"That this young . . . ah . . . cub is extremely talented." The tall man held out one of Isabella's drawings. "Look at this, Jean, instead of the child's anatomy."

Maillot spluttered. "You looby, can't you see—"

"His costume is most objectionable, true, but I expect his mistress requires him to dress thusly for his employment, is that not so, Miss . . . ?" He turned to Virginia, once again raking her approvingly with his startling ice blue eyes.

"Douglas," Virginia hastened to inform him. Unaccountably flustered, she blushed beneath his gaze. "Virginia Douglas." As this tall stranger was the handsomest creature she had ever seen, Virginia quite forgot to use her mother's name.

"*Lady Douglas,* or so she told me," Maillot sneered.

"Oh!" Confusion pinked Virginia's cheeks even more. "I meant Lady Douglas, of course."

"Ha!" Maillot exploded. "Something dashed smoky about this business."

Isabella rushed to cover Virginia's gaffe. "You see, my mistress sent her daughter with me to seek a tutor, as she was so busy."

"Enough!" The irascible artist nearly roared. "Ladies, this fardiddle has gone too far. I do not teach females, no matter how talented, and no matter how cleverly disguised. My servant will see you to your carriage."

Isabella groaned. How had he known? She and Virginia had made sure her disguise was perfect. It had been enough to fool Virginia's servants, including the butler, who had only admonished "Clarence" to see his mistress did not go beyond their own square when told Virginia was going for a short walk. It had fooled the jarvey who had brought them here in a hired hackney cab. Why had it not fooled this temperamental artist?

Perhaps it was just a guess. Isabella drew herself up. "It is not kind of you, sir, to make fun of me just because I am chubby and my mistress dresses her pages in ruffles and lace. Please, Mr. Maillot. I wish to learn how to paint landscapes, and Lady Douglas was assured at the Royal Academy that you were the very one to teach me."

Virginia, guiltily aware that she had damaged Isabella's chances, hastily inserted, "And you shall not lose thereby, sir. Whatever your usual fee is, Isa . . . that is, my mother shall double it."

"You could double it to perdition and back and I would not teach a member of your sex, most particularly not a member of the quality. Now please go, or I shall have my servant—"

"Gently, Jean, gently. Perhaps we can assist this very talented young . . . ah . . . person by finding an appropriate tutor." The handsome blond turned to Virginia. "Allow me to introduce myself, as my volatile friend here has neglected to do so. I am Harrison Curzon, at your service."

He bowed respectfully to Virginia, then turned to Isabella. One brow arched, he asked her, "And what shall I call you?"

"Clarence, sir. I am Lady Douglas's page."

"Clarence." His mouth tugged upward. "Well, then, Clarence, let us see what you have brought us."

Hope welling up, Isabella took several more drawings from the heavy portfolio and handed them to Mr. Curzon. Then she gathered up those that had scattered and spread them along Mr. Maillot's worn brown sofa.

Observing how seriously Curzon studied the drawings and paintings scattered about the small, bare parlor, Jean Maillot began to look at them himself. He muttered as he walked about.

Finally, he turned to find Harrison and both young ladies awaiting his verdict eagerly. He threw up his hands. "Yes, she has ability. A great deal of ability. For a female. But she is trouble. *Trouble!* Any female is, a gently bred one even more so, and one who will dress up as a boy and come to a man's lodgings is the worst that can be imagined. Sooner would I teach the devil to paint than her."

"But I am not . . ."

"Give it up, Clarence." Curzon ruffled Bella's golden curls. "Your charade is over. Jean, if you will not take her on, whom do you recommend?"

Maillot frowned. "Curse you, Harry, just because you pay me a king's ransom to teach you, that doesn't give you the right to involve me—" Seeing that Curzon was beginning to look imperious, he stopped his diatribe. "Oh, very well. She should apply to Mr. Morgan. He specializes in teaching ladies."

An exasperated hiss escaped Isabella's lips. "I have already learned all of what he has to teach me."

Curzon snorted derisively. "And rather more, I should say. Jean, you know very well that all Morgan is capable of doing is turning out flower painters or insipid watercolorists. Miniatures for lockets are his pupils' highest attainments."

"And that is exactly what this one should be doing. You know my thoughts on female artists. And she wishes to paint landscapes. Landscapes! Pah! She'd have to climb on a scaffolding to paint a decent landscape."

Curzon laughed. "True."

Furious, Isabella clenched her fists. "I don't want to paint miniatures, and I've painted enough flowers to last me a lifetime. I want to paint full-length portraits and grand landscapes, and don't tell me I am too short, because Mr. J. M. W. Turner is very nearly of a height with me, and you won't tell him that he is too short, I'll vow!"

"What a ferocious page you have, Miss Douglas." Curzon looked in no way offended by Isabella's vehemence. "You are quite *rompéd,* Jean. Whom else do you suggest?"

"To say nothing of the danger to her feminine brain, do you really think an excellent teacher, an artist worthy of his salt, should waste his time on a female? Especially this female?"

"I do."

"Nonsense. You are just entertaining yourself with this peculiar situation."

"It *is* droll, but I am quite serious about helping her. Have you forgotten that two years ago you were just as vehemently declaring that no gentleman could or would become a serious artist? I believe you do not still think that?"

A sly look spread over Maillot's face. "I was wrong, there. You are coming along very well. Hmmm." He turned to face the two young ladies. "It so happens, Miss Douglas and Miss . . . Clarence, that I know just the person."

"You do?" Isabella clapped her hands. "Is he anywhere near as accomplished as you, sir? For I have heard that you will be the next great landscape artist."

"I may well achieve that title," Maillot responded without modesty. "Especially if I can distract the man who might be my rival, would he but stop wasting his time on portraiture! And you, Miss Clarence, might just be the very distraction that I need."

Eyes shining, Isabella drew near the dark-haired artist. "Oh, I do hope this paragon will take me on, for I also need instruction in figure drawing."

"He is one of England's foremost experts on the female figure, I do assure you." Maillot's tone of voice was insinuating. "He might well derive great pleasure from drawing that well-rounded derriere in those tight satin breeches."

Curzon stiffened. "Here, now, Jean. You are forgetting that we are dealing with ladies—very young ladies, at that."

"Just so, Harry. I know I'm no fit company for ladies, which is only one of many reasons why I must excuse myself from taking on this excellent pupil." Maillot turned back to Isabella, grinning broadly. "But the man I propose for you to engage is not only an excellent artist, but one of your own class as well."

"A member of the *ton*, give lessons?" Virginia's astonished voice expressed perfectly both girls' misgivings.

"You sneak!" Curzon scowled furiously at the short man grinning up at him.

Maillot took Isabella's hand. "Come, Miss Clarence. I will introduce you to your new teacher. Miss Clarence, Mr. Harrison Curzon. Harry, Miss Clarence, a most talented artist in need of instruction by a gentleman who appreciates the female mind almost as much as he does the female form."

He joined her hand to Curzon's, and then dashed nimbly from the room, leaving three stunned people in his wake.

Chapter Three

Isabella was sufficiently unnerved by the feel of Harrison Curzon's large hand engulfing hers that she said nothing for several moments. He stared wordlessly down at her, as if he were equally bemused by the situation.

Isabella spoke first. "Are you really a good artist?"

"Single-minded little creature." Curzon released her hand and unceremoniously dropped into a nearby chair.

"Hadn't you best inquire if I am really a gentleman, first?"

"I never expected nor required that my teacher be a gentleman, nor do I care a fig for it now, so long as he is a capable teacher who is willing to take a female artist seriously. But I collect you are but a gentleman painter, sir, and Mr. Maillot has had his fun at my expense." Suddenly overwhelmed by the hopelessness of her situation, she dropped several silent tears before stopping them by scrubbing her eyes vigorously.

"I am so sorry, Bella." Virginia put her arm around Bella and patted her shoulder consolingly. "At least we did try. Come, we must leave before we are missed."

Isabella pulled away from her and turned her back on them both, fighting for composure.

Poor mite. It means so much to her. Curzon felt an unfamiliar emotion. It wasn't entirely pity, nor even sympathy. It was a feeling of connection that he had never experienced with anyone else. He understood the child's unhappiness so very well. She really cared about art, just as he did, always had since the day he could first grasp a colored chalk in his hand. She really had talent, as he fancied he had. And her case was even more hopeless than his, for as *outré* as a serious male artist was among the *ton,* a truly serious female artist from their class was unheard of, and obviously those who were in charge of her education meant to see that it remained so, else she would not have had to engage in this charade.

Collecting herself, Isabella turned back to face him. "Wait, Ginny. Mr. Curzon hasn't answered yet."

"Answered what?" Lost in his own thoughts, Curzon had forgotten Isabella's question.

"*Are* you a tolerable artist, sir, or just a Sunday painter?" Her skeptical expression challenged him.

Annoyed, Curzon leaned forward. "Would you like to see for yourself, midget?"

"Yes, I would!"

He stood. "Well, then, I will take you to my studio."

"No," Virginia protested. "We can't go anywhere with him, Bella. That would be too much."

"It will be unexceptionable, Virginia. I am here to chaperone you—"

Virginia and Curzon let out nearly identical rude snorts at this assertion.

"Is your studio nearby?"

"Nothing if not persistent, aren't you, little one? It is nearer than you can guess. I keep a loft right here above Maillot's, where I can paint undisturbed. A few steps will take us there."

He wasn't surprised when the diminutive blond child eagerly told him, "Lead on, sir."

Second thoughts assailed Harrison. It was perhaps not the wisest course to entice two innocents to his private lair. When he turned to Virginia, he deliberately let a seductive smile play along his lips as he offered her his arm. *She will cry off,* Curzon thought. *No gently bred female is going to climb those stairs to a loft with a man she's only just met.*

Virginia did not disappoint him. She shrank back. "Isabella, I don't think it would be proper—"

"Pooh! I thought better of you! Turning into a milk-and-water miss now, are you? Well, wait here, then!" Bella took Curzon's arm and all but pulled him from the room. Her eagerness was infectious. Harrison grinned and let himself be commandeered.

Virginia protested, "You can't go alone. That would be even worse. Wait . . ."

But the two had already reached the door to the central hallway and turned toward the stairs. Virginia scurried after them.

"Wonderful!" Isabella lifted her arms above her head and turned around in the huge, brilliantly lit room at the top of the stairs. "North light *and* a skylight. And so beautifully appointed. No one would guess it to see this building from the outside."

"Well, I don't like to paint in squalor." Curzon smiled at the small blonde.

"And these!" Dropping her arms, Isabella looked around her in fascination. The walls were lined with paintings in various stages of completion, some framed, but most still on their stretchers. "Never say you painted these magnificent canvases!"

"Guilty, I am afraid." Curzon slanted a glance at the lovely redhead. He was pleased that the little miss was impressed. He hoped her beautiful friend would be, as well.

Virginia, too, was staring around the room, but her emotion was deep embarrassment. Several of the paintings were female studies, distinguished to her mind more by their lack of clothing than their artistic merit.

"Bella, we *must* go!"

Abruptly, Bella marched toward the door. "Yes, we must. It is all a hum. He is only a copyist, and certainly no gentleman, for a gentleman would not lie and claim as his the compositions of others!"

Much nettled, Curzon sprang to block her way. "Just what do you mean by that remark?"

"That study propped against the wall. Doubtless you did not think I would have seen the original." Full of indignation, Bella shook a scolding finger at the man who towered over her. "It is called 'Their Mistress's Bonnets.' Lord Langley is a friend of mine, and he purchased it after the Royal Academy's annual exhibit two years ago. It hangs over his fireplace! I cannot remember just now who painted it, but—"

"Ah, is Lord Langley the one who bought it? I had my agent handle the sale, as I must remain anonymous. Mustn't embarrass the family, you know. That's why I didn't sign it."

The disdain began to fade from Isabella's face. "You are telling me that *you* created that wonderful painting?"

He bowed to her. "I am pleased that one of your ability praises it."

Her eyes searched his. "Truly? You truly did?"

Flattered in spite of himself by the worshipful tone and the awe in her eyes, Curzon inclined his head.

She lifted her hands prayerfully. "That is of all things wonderful. In that case, you may indeed teach me. When shall we start?"

"I may teach you! But I never said . . ."

Horror spread over Isabella's expressive face. "Oh, never say you are going to cry off. Don't snatch this joy away from me!"

"Emotional little thing, ain't you!" But Curzon again felt that odd sweep of emotion himself. He understood all too well her intense need.

"How could it be done? You are too young to go about on your own, and obviously your family does not wish you to further your studies."

"That's not true. My grandmother had hoped to hire Mr. Maillot to instruct me, but he would not because I am female, so she engaged Mr. Morgan. She had the best of intentions, because he is accounted a thoroughly respectable man. She simply does not understand his lack of qualification to teach me. But now I've found you. You are not only a marvelous artist, you are a gentleman. She will be pleased to have you tutor me. Could you call on us tomorrow?"

Curzon shook his head vehemently. "You are thinking only of yourself, *enfant*. Haven't you been listening to me? I don't even sign my paintings. Few know how serious I am about my art, because it would expose me, and hence my family, to ridicule. How, then, could I present myself to your grandmother as a qualified teacher?"

"We will bring her here, let her see your paintings."

Harrison shook his head. "It wouldn't serve."

"Why?"

Curzon cleared his throat. He didn't know who this little chit's family was, but her perfect diction and her friendship with the exquisite Miss Douglas marked her as a member of his own class. His reputation was such that he seriously doubted he would be allowed to teach her. He felt embarrassed to explain about such disreputable considerations to these two innocent young females, however.

"I don't want my artistic pretensions revealed to the mocking eye of the *ton*, I tell you. We will have to find some other teacher."

"I don't want another teacher! I want you. I will just have to come to you here, then."

"As Miss Douglas has already pointed out to you, your presence here in my studio, unchaperoned, would cause a scandal did it become known."

"Then we shall just have to keep it a secret! I shall find a way! Virginia will help me. We managed to evade all our chaperones today, and we shall do it again, shan't we, Virginia?"

"Well, I . . ."

Isabella confronted her friend fiercely. "You must, you simply must help me, or I'll never speak to you again!"

Curzon knew he should refuse to participate in this scheme. Yet as he looked from the desperate child to her hesitant friend, he found that he wanted to help her more than he wanted to avoid scandal. Another thought drew him into the plot as well. *I could paint this beauty while teaching her friend*, he realized. *Green eyes, peaches-and-cream complexion.* His mind was already moving over what colors his palette would require to capture that delicate skin.

Curzon moved to Virginia's side. "Do not fail us, fair maiden." He raised her trembling hands to his lips and kissed one, then the other. "I shall welcome your presence as much as I welcome the opportunity to nurture this budding young Angelica Kaufman. I hope to paint your portrait while instructing her."

Faced with Bella's heated insistence and the magnetic presence of this handsome man, Virginia wordlessly nodded.

"Oh, famous!" Dancing about the room, Isabella took several moments to calm down enough for Virginia to remind her of the time.

"You are right. We mustn't be late. Mustn't be caught now! We'll return on . . . let me see . . . Thursday, sir. That is my grandmother's visiting day, and she can't stand to take me with her, for I can never sit still. What time would be most convenient?"

Never. Harry, this is your maddest start ever, he scolded himself. But he found himself saying out loud, "At noon?"

"Yes! And thank you, sir. Thank you so much!" Isabella fairly raced from the room before he could change his mind. Virginia hastened after her, leaving Harrison Curzon shaking his head in amazement at what he had just agreed to.

The young girls hastened to find a hackney to convey them back to Virginia's house. Once settled in the carriage, Virginia listened to Isabella's excited chatter with a distracted manner, her brow knitted, her finger tapping her lips thoughtfully. Just as they reached their destination, she interrupted the flow of Bella's words with a wail.

"Oh, why did I say yes? We can't go there again. We can't be alone with that man in his studio!"

"Why not, Ginny? He's a gentleman, born and bred. It might be a bit irregular, but we'll come to no harm."

"I shouldn't be at all sure of that, Bella. You see, when I heard his name, it seemed familiar to me. I just now realized who he is. He is as dangerous as he is handsome."

"Dangerous?"

"Yes, indeed. Gilbert mentioned him to me in the park the other day while we were driving around."

"Well, there you are, then. If he's a friend of Gilbert's, whom you said was all propriety, he must be perfectly acceptable."

Deliciously shivery at the thought, Virginia intoned, "That's just it! He mentioned Mr. Curzon while lecturing me about how to conduct myself in the season. One of the ones I should avoid, he said." Virginia paused dramatically, as Bella hung on her every word.

"A very dangerous man is Harrison Curzon. He is known as the Golden Rake!"

"The Golden Rake?" Bella's eyes widened. "That sounds terrible. At least I think it does. What exactly *is* a rake, Ginny?"

Ginny's brow crinkled. "I don't know, exactly. But I think it means he is inclined to behave improperly."

"Virginia Douglas! You won't have Lord Threlbourne because he is too dull and proper, yet here is a man who is neither dull nor proper, and obviously smitten with you, and yet you don't want to have anything to do with him, either!"

"Oh! That is true." Virginia put one hand to her mouth. "This will be an adventure to remember, won't it? And after all, he cannot be so very bad, for he scolded Mr. Maillot for leering at you."

"That's right. Now, you must begin to think hard, for how we are to escape everyone's notice frequently enough for me to profit from his tutelage I cannot imagine, yet it must be done!"

"Thank you for coming so promptly, Harry." Sir Randall Curzon motioned his oldest son to sit down next to him on a wrought iron chair. They were on the south porch at The Elms, looking out over the magnificent vista that Capability Brown had created. A Greek temple shimmered in the morning mist across the lake.

"It isn't far to come," Harrison responded, smiling. "But an hour or so in my curricle, after all."

"Far enough that you haven't been here for three months," his father ground out, mitigating the complaint with a rueful smile.

"True." Harrison waited. From long experience he knew that whatever it was that his father had summoned him here to discuss would not be hurried by any questions or signs of impatience on his part.

"How is that sorrel team working out?"

"Well enough. Not as fast as the blacks were, but steadier in town traffic."

"Now there is a change, you caring about steadiness. Could it be that you are growing up at last, my boy?"

"What a ghastly thought!"

His father flashed an appreciative smile, but quickly sobered. "It is about growing up that I have asked you here today, Harry."

"That sounds ominous." Harrison tugged on his left ear as he was wont to do when worried or upset.

"Perhaps you will think it so. I had hoped that someday soon you would voluntarily give up this childish notion of devoting yourself to art, but if anything, in the last two years you have spent even more of your time and energy on this chimera."

"*Is* it a chimera, sir? Several fellow artists have said I might take first prize in the exhibition, if only I would permit my paintings to compete."

"And what is the point of it? You don't need the money, and the prestige it would bring to a needy artist would only be embarrassing to you and your family."

"Lord Byron does not blush to sell his poems, nor to sign his name to them."

"Hardly the most felicitous defense, Harry. Byron needs the money; you do not. Byron cares nothing for his reputation, for he has none. And he has already hurt his family as much as it is possible for him to do."

Harrison sighed. There was no point in trying to defend the indefensible. "I have no wish to hurt you, sir. That is why I have insisted on remaining anonymous."

"But you are selling paintings. Unless I am very much mistaken, there is one of yours hanging in Lord Langley's drawing room. You don't even know the man, so you could hardly have given it to him."

Harrison swallowed hard. How unfortunate that one of his few sales should have been to Lord Langley. Of course his father would visit the salon of one of leaders of political reform. "I have sold a few paintings anonymously, through an agent," he admitted.

"Why? With the allowance I make you, you cannot be wanting money. Unless ... see here, Harry, you haven't taken up wild gaming again?"

"No, Pater. It is just that my many relatives and friends have all been the recipients of my paintings *ad nauseam*. After painting them, I have an irresistible desire to display them, to know that they are seen. Besides, I know they are truly valued when someone is willing to pay for them. In the case of Langley's painting, he valued it quite highly!"

"It is an exceptionally handsome painting. I would have been honored to give it house room. Did it ever occur to you that you are taking bread from the mouths of other artists?"

Harrison hung his head. "Yes, sir."

"Harry, I have always been a generous—some might even say an indulgent—father."

"I have never wanted for anything," Harrison acknowledged.

"Except for responsibilities. I have decided that you would benefit from having respectable employment. Lord Langley has at last persuaded me to take a more active role in politics. I am thinking about purchasing a pocket borough near Stone Wicket."

Harrison looked warily at his father. "What has this to do with me?"

"I want you to stand for the House of Commons. I've a mind to have a voice in the struggle for reform. In time I might go ahead and make the investment in a title. With me in the House of Lords and you in the Commons, we can help bring about some much needed changes in our system of government, including the abolition of pocket boroughs."

Harrison Curzon scrambled to his feet. "Politics! Never! Waste my time listening to boring speeches, planning boring speeches of my own, plotting and planning and scheming. Never, never, never!"

Sir Randall stood, too. "I was afraid that would be your reaction. In that case, I shall go ahead immediately and make the loan that will gain me a title. Our expensive new king is as short of the ready now as he ever was as Prince Regent, and will overlook my politics for a loan with sufficiently generous terms. But the consequence is, I shall be busy in the House of Lords. Our estates and other investments will need attending to. You must take them over and manage them for me. And believe me, my boy, there will be precious little time left over for painting!"

Harrison stared at his father, not quite believing what he was hearing. "Me, a farmer? There is nothing I despise more than tramping over fields . . ."

"You didn't balk at a two-month walking tour in the north country. Nor yet at a year tramping around Europe, climbing the Alps."

"That was different, Pater. I was painting. I love trying to capture the lighting on a mountain peak. Or the roses on a woman's cheeks. But trying to decide whether to grow wheat or turnips—no! I don't know a drain from a drill press . . ."

"You'll learn, Harry. You always were a bright lad."

"I don't care to learn, sir. If it must be one or the other, I suppose it must be politics."

"Excellent. Don't look so glum. I have an idea that some responsibilities will be the making of you. Oh, and while we are discussing your future, it's time for you to marry. You have had two years to get over that fiasco with Miss Gresham. Time to look about you again. As well you didn't marry the Gresham chit. Obscure country gentry, hardly a suitable wife for a politician. Pelham was a right fool to make such a *mésalliance*. You need a wife from one of the first families, one who knows how to serve as a hostess and run a great house."

Harrison pulled fiercely on his earlobe, his face a pained grimace. "That's even more unlikely than my becoming a farmer. Gently bred females and I are like oil and water."

"If you didn't spend so much time with your pretty Cyprians, you'd soon learn how to go on."

"Insipid little milk-and-water misses take alarm at my wooing, sir."

"You are wealthy—"

"I am your pensioner, in truth."

"And handsome, more handsome than is good for you, and soon to be the heir to a title. You can find a well-connected wife. If you can't, I will find one for you!"

Harrison looked at his father's determined face with a sinking feeling. He had always gotten along well with his parents, particularly this man who stood before him, who unlike many aristocratic fathers had taken a great interest in his son, teaching him to ride and hunt and shoot, and taking a certain perverse pride in the boy's wild career as a man-about-town. Harrison not only owed him filial obedience, he loved him and wished not to come in conflict with him. But this . . . this was too much!

He began shaking his head. "Sir, I really don't think you have chosen the right son for this role. What about Patrick? He is fascinated by politics."

"Huh! The more radical, the better. I want reform, not revolution. No, Patrick is just a boy, still working out the fidgets. I hope he won't take as long about it as you, but I can't wait. Besides, the title, and therefore the political power, will go to you, so it should be you who gains the experience to deal with it." Sir Randall clamped a hand on his son's shoulder in what was meant as a comforting gesture.

"You'll adjust, my boy. I have great confidence in you. I'm glad you made the decision you did."

"Decision, sir? More like accepting an edict."

"Not at all. You may choose. The House of Commons, or gentleman farmer. Take a little while, if you wish, to think about it. You'll let me know in, shall we say, a month's time? Now come and greet your mother and grandmother. They are delighted to have you visit after so long."

Chapter Four

The drive back to London gave Harrison Curzon some time for reflection. He had no wish to come to cuffs with his father, and not just because Sir Randall held the purse strings. *I have led a charmed existence, thus far. A parasitical existence, in truth*, Harry scolded himself. *I've always cared more for the cut of my coat and the speed of my horses than the source of my income. Pater is right. I've spent too long playing at being an artist. Just because it fascinates me does not mean it is right to paint to the exclusion of all else.*

He was unable, however, to decide which of the two alternatives his father had offered him would be the least distasteful to him. *I expect the first thing is to look about me for a wife.* Though not distasteful, neither was it, Harrison knew, a simple task. A little more than two years ago he had courted a lovely country-bred maiden with dusky curls and rosy cheeks, but his aggressive wooing had frightened her, and she had wed another.

It's as Pater said. I've spent too many years among the muslin company, he acknowledged ruefully. *Most gently bred females seem boring by comparison. And even if I find another one to interest me, can I win her, or will she turn from me in disgust when I make love to her?*

He was distracted in these ruminations by the sight of a curricle moving toward him. It was moved smartly along by a pair of matched grays. He knew those grays, and their owner, Gilbert Douglas, Lord Threlbourne. *But here is fortune, smiling on me!* Harrison's eyes lit as he recognized the fair charmer sitting beside Threlbourne. *By all the saints! It is the lovely redhead who attempted to pass off that child as her page!*

"Ho, Gil!" Harrison drew up his team. Politeness dictated that Threlbourne stop his curricle in turn, but the look on his face spoke of deep reluctance to do so.

"Harry." Threlbourne nodded curtly as he brought his steaming horses to a halt.

"Were you on your way to The Elms, Gil? If so, I almost missed you."

"Just taking a drive in the country, Harry. Bid you good day." He lifted his reins, obviously eager to move on.

"But aren't you going to introduce me to this lovely miss by your side?" Curzon grinned, amused by the discomfiture of both redheads. Threlbourne's complexion had become almost as red as his carrot-colored locks. The peach tones of Virginia's skin had deepened, too, as she looked in panic at the man who might expose her misdeeds.

With no good grace, Threlbourne introduced Virginia to Harrison, who tipped his hat politely.

"Enchanted, Miss Douglas. So you are Gilbert's intended. I am beginning to see why he has waited for you for so long. Are we to expect an announcement soon?"

Rebellion brought Virginia out of her embarrassed silence. She snapped, "We are not engaged, nor planning to be, Mr. Curzon. Just because our parents thought we should wed, does not mean that as adults we must conform to their wishes."

Harry lifted in interrogative eyebrow at Gil. "Beg pardon, Miss Douglas. Gil has spoken of you so often. I assumed—"

Virginia jammed her elbow into Gilbert's side, forcing him to admit, "No, Harry, we're not engaged. Virginia has decided that we will not suit. My cousin, though. Mean to see she manages her entry into the *ton* without taking any harm."

This was clearly intended to warn Curzon off, but had no effect. Instead, he leaned forward eagerly. "Excellent. Then pray do say, Miss Douglas, that I may call on you soon."

The ice blue eyes, snapping with glee, held hers. Virginia had little choice but to agree, not that she minded in the least. Discomfiting Gilbert was not her only reason for responding with pleasure. Harrison Curzon was handsome as sin, and as Isabella had pointed out, not likely to be as stuffy as her cousin.

"I should be honored, sir. We are at home on Friday afternoon, as it happens." Ignoring Gilbert's muttering and grumbling at her side, she gave Curzon her direction and flicked him a flirtatious smile as they parted.

Very well done indeed, Harrison congratulated himself as he continued on his way to London. *It must be fate, to present me just at this time with a ravishing female who is well-connected and attracted to me, too, unless I miss my guess.* Her daring participation in the adventure with the faux page suggested that Virginia Douglas might be a freer spirit than Davida Gresham. Perhaps she was just the wife he needed!

Virginia could not wait to apprise Isabella of this fortuitous introduction. She had Gilbert deliver her to the duchess's town house and instructed him to go on without her. "Isabella and her companion Miss Fenton will walk me home, or the duchess will send me in her carriage. Run along, Gilbert, do!"

After seeing her safely into the duchess's drawing room, Lord Threlbourne stiffly bid her a good day. She had quarreled bitterly with him on the way home, for he had tried to tell her she might not see Harrison Curzon.

She had responded, "I take exception to your choosing my suitors for me, Gilbert Douglas! You don't own me, nor ever shall."

"I know I don't, but I care what happens to you, and to further your acquaintance with Harrison Curzon is not at all the thing."

But she had turned a deaf ear to his remonstrances and had huffily urged him, "Take me back to town as soon as may be, for I have no pleasure in your company when you are in such a dictatorial mood."

He had done so, not deigning to speak to her again. Eager to be private with Bella, Virginia was pleased when the duchess, who was receiving visitors, told her that her granddaughter was upstairs.

"Bella, Bella, you'll never guess. Now I know how your lessons may be arranged," she exclaimed, bursting into Isabella's studio.

"Ginny! You startled me so that I spattered crimson all over my mountain," Bella grumbled.

"Never mind that. I know how—" Virginia stopped and looked all around her. "Miss Fenton isn't nearby, is she?" Bella's companion, Mary Fenton, usually wrote poetry while her charge painted.

"No, she is at the Langleys', showing Lady Langley a new poem." Curiosity overcame Bella's annoyance. "Just let me wipe out this mess and clean my brushes, and we shall have a comfortable coze."

A few moments later she joined the impatient Virginia on a small sofa. "Now tell me what has you in such an uproar."

"I met Harrison Curzon today."

"You met him Monday, silly."

"No, I mean really met him. A formal introduction, during our drive in the country today. Gil was livid to be forced into doing the honors! And then Mr. Curzon asked permission to call on me."

A frown line appeared between Bella's eyebrows. "That is wonderful if you are interested in furthering your acquaintance with the man, but I am not sure how it helps me, Ginny . . ."

"But it does. I've come up with a perfect scheme. You

know how perplexed you were as to how we could elude everyone often enough for you to get any real benefit from his tutelage?"

"Especially Miss Fenton. She was most perturbed when she found that we were not at your home when she came back for me Monday. She said if I went off alone again, she would tell my grandmother."

"Now that I've been properly introduced to Mr. Curzon, we can ask him to paint my portrait. That will give us an excuse to visit him. Your companion can accompany us, which means your grandmother and my mother both will be satisfied."

Bella bounced joyfully on the sofa. "You clever girl!" Her glee quickly faded, though. "Didn't you say that he is not quite the thing? Do you really think my grandmother and your mother will permit us to go to the studio of someone called the Golden Rake?"

Virginia put her index finger in her mouth and rotated it, chewing anxiously on the nail. "My mother might, if we were properly chaperoned, but the duchess is such a high stickler . . ."

A gloomy silence settled over the room as both girls thought about the problem. At last Bella brightened. "What about this. We'll tell Mary it is to be a surprise. You want to give your mother and father a portrait for their anniversary, but you can't afford Reynolds. Mr. Curzon has offered to do it for free, but it must be kept secret, because he doesn't want his artistsc endeavors known."

Floundering, Bella waited for further inspiration.

"Would your companion know about Mr. Curzon's reputation?"

Bella wrinkled her nose. "I'm not sure. She knows little of the *ton*. Perhaps not. She would be intrigued and sympathetic with a gentleman who wishes to paint seriously. I am sure that if she can be persuaded to take us there, she will agree to let me study with him, for she is quite protective of me and encourages my ambitions."

"Then we shall just have to try her."

"I will put it to her this evening." Bella leaned forward and hugged Virginia. "Thank you ever so much. How thankful I am that your family brought you to London now! I don't think there are many other girls who would be willing to enter such a scheme with me!"

Harrison Curzon began cleaning his brushes. It was two o'clock and his "pupil" had not appeared. He wasn't surprised. The child, surely not above ten or twelve, would doubtless find it extremely difficult to escape from the schoolroom a second time. Even if that were not the case, since Gilbert would have lost no time in warning Miss Douglas away from him, she probably wouldn't even be willing to continue the adventure.

His mouth quirked as he thought of how alarmed Miss Douglas must have been when she learned that the man whose studio she had visited unchaperoned by any but a child was known in the *ton* as the Golden Rake. *I earned that sobriquet*, he thought regretfully. *Once upon a time I was even proud of it.*

It had been a good painting session this morning. As he did every morning, Curzon had begun painting long before most men of his age and social class were even awake in London. Now it was almost time to put in an appearance at one or more of those activities that had earned him the reputation of being a Corinthian, a nonesuch, a pink of the *ton*.

Curzon stood back to study his work, a large painting of three people: a flower girl, her customer, and a toddler clinging to her skirts. Maillot would call it sentimental rubbish, for the mother's penury and the child's ragged appearance contrasted sharply with the magnificent dress of the dandy, who leered suggestively at the flower girl as he bought a posy.

It still needed a great deal of work, but he felt good about it. *There are more ways to expose the sins of excessive wealth than speeches in Parliament*, he thought. Stretching his arms above his head, he yawned mightily. His unbuttoned cuffs dropped down, exposing muscular forearms dusted with curling gold hair.

It was thus that Isabella beheld him as she paused in the doorway to his studio. Her breath caught in her throat. *He is gorgeous*, she thought. *I wish I could paint him.*

Behind her, Miss Mary Fenton gasped. This was the "nice young gentleman" who had agreed to paint Virginia's portrait, and whom Bella hoped would give her art instruction! The phrase had suggested a polite, kind, tame sort of creature. The reality was a stunningly handsome man, tall, strongly built, and giving more than a hint of leashed masculine power that she found most alarming. Instantly, she regretted agreeing to come here.

"Isabella, I don't think . . ." she began to whisper in her charge's ear.

To forestall her, Virginia quickly proceeded into the room. "Good afternoon, Mr. Curzon. I am so sorry to be late, but it was very difficult to get away. First Bella's grandmother had to come in to talk to Mama, to be quite sure Bella had been properly invited, and then we must all take tea with her before we could leave. Do say it isn't too late."

Curzon dropped his arms. "Ladies, forgive my undress." In two long strides he retrieved his coat and drew it on. As he did so, he took a second look at Isabella, whom he had not immediately recognized. She was charmingly gowned in a delft blue walking dress, clutching a small canvas to her bosom. A very shapely bosom it was, too.

With difficulty he managed not to betray his astonishment at discovering that the golden-haired "child" of two days before, no longer dressed as a page, was a woman. Young, to be sure, and petite, but very definitely a woman, with enormous, vivid blue eyes and full, kissable lips in a sweetly rounded face.

Virginia led Bella and the other woman forward, her eyes signaling him for cooperation as she did so. "This is my dear friend Isabella Eardley, and her companion, Miss Fenton, who has agreed to chaperone me as I sit for my portrait. And please let me say again how grateful I am that you have offered to paint it as a surprise anniversary gift for my parents."

Eyes shining with admiration for whoever had devised this excuse, Curzon bowed politely to Miss Fenton and Isabella. "You are Virginia's friend who also aspires to be an artist, I believe," he said, taking the opportunity to study Isabella's curvaceous form appreciatively.

Bella curtsied to him, relieved that he had taken them up so quickly. "Yes, sir. Virginia said you might agree to critique some of my paintings. I have brought one today, which I know needs extensive work on perspective."

Mary Fenton curtsied nervously. This man was too attractive, and the look in his eyes too knowing, for her to be comfortable with him. "Bella, I am not sure—"

"Mary, please! I shan't bother Mr. Curzon very much. He will have plenty of time to paint Virginia. And look! Here is a comfortable chair and a writing desk. You may work on your poetry while we are painting!" Taking the hesitant companion by her hand, Isabella drew the older woman across the room.

"Yes, please be assured, Miss Fenton, that I do not mind instructing your charge. I know firsthand how difficult it is for a member of the gentry to pursue a serious interest in art. I can imagine that it is even more difficult for a young girl than it is for a man."

His expression was sincere. Mary allowed herself to be

persuaded, and settled down with her current project. Curzon winked at Bella before leading Virginia to a raised platform. There he placed her in a comfortable chair and draped her with a swath of pale green satin. He resisted the urge to flirt with her, sensing her uneasiness at having him so near.

He already had a stretched canvas set up on a nearby easel. Bella watched in fascination as he began sketching Virginia in much-diluted burnt sienna. After he had worked for a while, he glanced over and saw that Mary was entirely engrossed in her poetry.

"Well, Clarence, you are full of surprises," he said in a low voice, continuing his sketching as he did so.

"It was Virginia's idea; isn't she clever?"

"I meant, my dear, that I thought you were a child. I was expecting my pupil to be at the most, twelve."

She looked at him anxiously. "I know that I look very young, but I am almost eighteen. You don't mind that I am not a child, do you?"

"Perhaps. Children learn so much faster than adults." Seeing the gathering distress in Bella's large blue eyes, he grinned. "Never mind. I shan't tease you. Set your canvas up, and I'll give you a few hints."

She did as he bade her, watching and listening intently as he discussed perspective with her, marking lightly on the canvas with charcoal as he did so.

"I recognize this scene. It is Braughing, in Hertfordshire, isn't it?"

"Yes. It is one of our few picturesque views. Is it very bad?"

"Not bad at all. As I said the other day, you are undeniably gifted." He stood back. "Do you understand what needs to be done?"

She nodded enthusiastically. "I plan to have canvas, brushes, and colors delivered here before we come next time. I know you won't want me using your materials."

Returning to his sketch of the now fidgeting Virginia, Curzon shook his head. "I don't mind, infant. Don't risk exposing your misdeeds for something so trivial. There is an already stretched canvas against the wall if you wish to begin now." He glanced back at her. "I collect you won't want to risk ruining that gown, though."

"Oh, I quite forgot a smock. I will certainly have one of those sent over. But I can begin my sketch, if you will lend me some charcoal."

They worked quietly side by side in the light streaming from the windows and skylight for almost an hour before Virginia moaned and stretched. "I do hate to stop you, but I am beginning to cramp in places I didn't know I had muscles."

Curzon put down his brush and helped her from the chair in which he had placed her. "I beg your pardon. I should have given you a break much sooner. Walk around and stretch a bit. Do you think you will be able to go for a drive with me tomorrow?"

Flustered by his nearness and his warm regard, Virginia backed away slightly. "It is the oddest thing. My mother was all for refusing to allow you to call on me, but Gilbert, to my surprise, urged her to agree. Perhaps if you are all propriety during your call . . ."

"Let us hope she does not discover this little tête-à-tête, then." Harry grinned as his eyes scanned the room. Bella was sketching intently, the tip of her tongue protruding from the left side of her rosebud mouth. Miss Fenton, head down, was scribbling furiously. He and Virginia were, to all intents and purposes, quite alone.

"No, that would never do!" Virginia returned his smile, but retreated yet another step. "I expect we had best leave, Bella. We have stretched what was supposed to be a visit to the stationers about as far as it will go."

Reluctantly putting down her charcoal, the petite blonde

wiped her hands briskly. "You are right. Besides, we have imposed on Mr. Curzon quite enough for one day. When may we come again, sir?"

"I paint every day until around 1:00. If you wish to come again this late, though, we had best plan ahead."

Mary had roused herself. "Mornings will be altogether easier to arrange," she said, standing up and gathering her scattered papers. "Her Grace sleeps late and generally relies on me to chaperone Bella before two."

"Her Grace?" Curzon froze in the act of draping a cloth over his sketch of Virginia.

Isabella bit her lower lip. "Oh, Mary!"

"Who *is* your grandmother? I thought the name was Eardley?" Curzon frowned ominously.

"My grandmother on my mother's side, sir. My mother was a Lacey."

"A Lacey?" Curzon searched his knowledge of the *ton*. "Not, surely, a relation of Richard Lacey, the Duke of Carminster?"

She tipped her small, round chin up and nodded, meeting his eyes squarely. "The duke is my uncle."

"My God! Your grandmother is the Dowager Duchess of Carminster?"

Chapter Five

"Yes." It took all of Bella's considerable courage to keep from shrinking away from the young giant who towered over her, looking very angry.

Curzon gave a short, harsh laugh and strode away to the northern window, scowling down into the busy street.

Bella bit her lip again. Usually words didn't fail her, but she knew she was asking something outrageous to expect anyone, especially a member of her own class, to risk offending the dowager, who was a leading member of society.

Virginia looked sympathetically at her friend as Curzon scowled and strode back toward them, saying "It is impossible. Quite, quite impossible."

"Please do not say so. I have learned so much in just this one short lesson. I will take up my disguise again, and come alone, and—"

"That would be even worse!" Curzon tugged on his left ear.

Great tears began to roll down Bella's cheek, though she did not weep or plead. She stood staring up at him hopelessly.

Curzon felt once again, and stronger than ever, that deep empathy that had embarked him on this mad adventure in the first place. Resisting its pull, he shook his head.

"I am sorry, young ladies, but I greatly fear should your grandmother learn who I am. . . . Her concern for the proprieties is legendary." His handsome face flushed, and once again Harrison Curzon wished he had been a little more discreet in his amours.

Mary Fenton spoke softly, unexpectedly, into the ensuing silence. "Your behavior today has been unexceptionable. I see no reason for the duchess to find out, but if she does, I shall assure her that you were all that a gentleman should be."

Curzon lowered his head, thinking. He really wanted to help the little blonde. And he was most eager to continue painting the beautiful redhead, whose ravishing coloration challenged his skills. And it wasn't as if he would seduce either of them, for he knew what was due to such well-born females. Why should he quail at the duchess's censure? After all, what could she do to him except express her displeasure?

"Very well. We shall contrive to avoid detection, but if we are discovered, we shall all take the position that Miss Fenton's chaperonage seemed quite sufficient. I fear, however, that you, Miss Fenton, will be the loser thereby, if we are discovered."

"No, she won't!" Isabella was suddenly fierce. "I have a generous allowance, and am quite an heiress in my own right. If Mary is discharged on my account, I will support her, at least until she can find other employment."

Miss Fenton put her arm around Isabella. "Lord Langley calls her Missy Boadicea. I think you see why, Mr. Curzon. Yes, I will help her, for she deserves her chance, and I fear before very much longer society will close its iron jaws around her."

"You make me shudder, Miss Fenton." But Curzon could only agree with the companion. Poor little Isabella's life would soon be forced into the only mold society provided for well-born females. Though he had never much concerned himself with the subject of women's rights, in this determined little creature's case, it seemed a shame that her future was so restricted.

"Then you will do it!" Virginia seemed much pleased. "I knew you were not stuffy! Would that more gentlemen had a sense of adventure!"

Miss Fenton looked anxiously at the clock on the mantel. "Girls, we had best be on our way, or we shall make mice feet of this particular adventure before we have well begun."

Curzon, you have run mad, he thought as he ushered the three women down to the street, where an elegant brougham awaited them. Yet he felt oddly elated and full of anticipation at the thought of Bella's next lesson.

"Lady Douglas, it is such a fine day, I wonder if you would permit me to take Miss Douglas for a ride in the park?" Harrison set down the delicate china teacup and looked hopefully at his hostess.

Virginia's mother nodded her head graciously. She had some reservations about this young man, but he seemed very nicely mannered, and of course one could not ignore his family or the fortune he would one day inherit.

"That would be splendid. After today, Virginia will be spending a great deal of time indoors. Her friend Isabella's governess has designed an impressive programme of education that involves visiting the significant buildings in the city and studying their history and architecture. They have kindly invited Virginia to join them."

Ginny caught at her lower lip with her teeth to keep from laughing out loud at the glee in Curzon's eyes as he expressed his admiration at their plans. "Do you care for architecture, Mr. Curzon?"

"It is one of my passions, Miss Douglas. Perhaps after our airing in the park I can take you to Somerset House, which in addition to housing the art school and paintings of all sorts, is a building of considerable architectural interest."

"I should like that excessively," she murmured.

Virginia admired Mr. Curzon's curricle as he assisted her into her seat. It was mahogany picked out in gold trim, and the sorrels' harnesses flashed with gold in the afternoon light.

"I expect your team is very fast, for I have heard that you are a Corinthian, sir." She fluttered her eyelashes at him as he took his seat and gathered the reins while his tiger ran to jump onto the back.

"Actually, this particular team is more suited to town driving than to racing."

"But I had heard that you beat all comers in curricle races."

He grinned. "I've won my share, that's true."

"Gilbert said you defeated both him and Lord Pelham once."

"Luck was with me that day. Pelham was distracted by lovesickness, and Gil was hampered by unfamiliarity with the course."

"You are too modest. I do wish I had seen it! Do you share my cousin Gilbert's love of boxing, sir? And of fencing?"

"Won't you call me Harry, and give me the freedom of your name?"

Virginia pinked at his warm look, but nodded her head.

"Yes, I fence, and box a round or two with Gentleman Jackson. Painting is a sedentary activity, so I like to stay fit." He flicked his team up as they entered Hyde Park. "Not many people about. Town is very thin of company as yet. Pity. I should like all of the fashionable *monde* to see me with such an exquisite beauty at my side." He caught up her gloved hand and bestowed a kiss on it, his eyes on her face as he did so.

Eyelashes fluttering again, Virginia remonstrated. "You'll make me conceited, sir. Tell me, do you truly think my friend Isabella is talented? She is so very intent on studying art, poor thing."

"Extremely talented. I know few female artists, so I scarce know who to compare her with, but she is certainly as good as many men now enrolled in the Academy."

"She is?" Virginia frowned.

"Does that bother you, Virginia?"

"I am concerned for her. A member of our class, and a female at that . . ."

Curzon's lips twisted. "It is not just females who find their pursuit of art frowned upon."

Virginia gave him a sympathetic look, and he soon found himself telling her of his father's attitude.

"It is a deal too bad, Harry, for him to try to tell you what you must do. I should think he would be proud of you. But could you not continue to paint and serve in Parliament? Or while managing his estates, for that matter?"

Curzon frowned. "It would become a mere hobby, then."

"Oh." She looked at him doubtfully. "That would not suffice?"

He sighed and looked away. "I suppose it will have to."

"Never say you are going to permit him to dictate to you?"

Icy eyes speared her. "You expect me to defy him? It is difficult to do, particularly when one's parent holds the purse strings."

She tilted her pointed chin up. "Gilbert did so. His father ordered him to marry me, and Gil told him he wouldn't if I didn't wish it. It was his staunch refusal to be manipulated that convinced my father to release me. He had shut me up in my room until I agreed to marry Gilbert."

"Ah, well, Gil is a courageous youth." Curzon smiled wryly. "Do you care for your cousin, Ginny?"

"Of course I do. We were raised as close as sister and brother. He is fond of me, too. But we don't love each other, and besides, I want someone less stuffy—someone less concerned for the proprieties, someone who isn't boring."

"Stuffy and boring. Now there are adjectives I would never have thought to apply to Gil. He is a nonesuch, you know. A first-class whip, admired by Jackson himself for his stylish footwork, the one swordsman who can give me an evenly matched bout, and looked to by all the young bucks seeking to be à la mode in their attire. A damn good drinking companion, too. Ah, pardon me, I see I have offended you."

Curzon suppressed a grin. Virginia's eyes had widened progressively as he praised Gilbert, but she pokered up at the curse. *She has considerable care for the proprieties herself*, Curzon thought, remembering how hesitant she had been to enter his studio. Only the force of Isabella's personality had carried her into so improper a situation.

Thinking of Bella reminded him of his wish to take Virginia to Somerset House. He had mentioned architecture to her mother, but it was paintings he wished to show to Virginia, his paintings, now on exhibit. He turned his horses.

As they were exiting the park, they passed Lord Threlbourne, just turning in. Up beside him was a ravishing brunette, looking at him adoringly.

He pulled up his team. "Well met again, Gil. Imagine seeing you here today." His lips lifted in an insinuating smile.

Gilbert scowled at Curzon. "Oh, it's you, Harry. Ginny. May I present Miss Blessington? She's newly come to town to renew her wardrobe, having just left off mourning for her aunt."

"*Enchanté*, Miss Blessington. Curzon greeted the beauty appreciatively, but Ginny was cool.

"You had best not be following us, Gilbert Douglas. I shan't be shadowed by you, do you hear!"

"Don't be bacon-brained, Ginny. Forgot you were even going for a drive. Excuse us, Harry. Promised to show Delilah my grays' paces." Gilbert touched his hat impatiently and his team sprang away.

"Hmmmph. Delilah! A forward creature, don't you think? On a first-name basis already. Well, he didn't lose any time."

Harry shook his head. "You care more for him than you will admit."

"Not a bit!"

"In fact, you seem jealous."

"I most certainly am not. I just . . . worry about him. With his title and fortune, he is sure to be taken in by some grasping female."

"I wouldn't worry about Gil. He is awake on all suits." Harry tooled his team to Somerset House, some of his enthusiasm for the outing dimmed by this exchange. *I don't want to get involved with a woman who doesn't realize she loves another man*, he thought grimly.

"Words cannot express, Your Grace, just how fortunate I think it is that Virginia has met Isabella. She is so much improved in her behavior now, I might almost call her biddable."

The Dowager Duchess of Carminster inclined her gray head regally. "Isabella has benefited, too. The child is a rare handful! But since they have been going about together she has become a model of decorum. It is almost too good to be true." A pair of parallel vertical lines between the duchess's eyebrows appeared as she contemplated the startling but gratifying change in her usually volatile granddaughter.

"So I have thought of Virginia. We have Miss Fenton to thank for some of it. Imagine such young girls becoming so caught up in a scheme to study London's architecture."

Lady Douglas raised a transparent bone china cup to her lips, smiling. Virginia had been fortunate indeed, to be taken up by one of the foremost families in England. It was a pity Isabella's father was a cit—what a name, Eardley! But to be the granddaughter of any duke gave instant cachet. To be taken up by the granddaughter of the Dowager Duchess of Carminster, one of society's *grande dames*, meant that Virginia's opportunities to find a highly placed husband were greatly increased. Since it looked like the match between Gilbert and Virginia was entirely exploded, Lady Douglas knew that her days of matchmaking had begun.

As if hearing her thoughts, the dowager began questioning Lady Douglas about the proposed match between Virginia and Lord Threlbourne.

"It is my husband and Gilbert's father who were insisting on the match. Neither Gilbert's mother nor I have ever thought that these plans would be acceptable to our children, who have played together and fought together like siblings all of their lives. Gilbert seemed inclined to go along with the match, in a lukewarm sort of way, but as soon as Virginia realized what was being planned, she balked."

"A high-spirited girl like her would do so, no matter how propitious the match. She is fortunate that matters have improved so much since my girlhood. Now fathers cannot force their daughters to wed at their command."

"No," sighed Lady Douglas. "But they can certainly make everyone miserable if their demands are not met."

"You could as well be speaking of Eardley as of Hamilton and Sir Sherwood," the dowager said, shaking her head ruefully. "I am pleased to hear that Lord Threlbourne is available, as it were. Perhaps he and Bella might suit. I must find a decent young man with a title for Isabella, before Eardley can marry off to one of his disreputable cronies."

"She could not do better than Gilbert. Such a pity Ginny wouldn't have him." Lady Douglas sighed. Both women contemplated the perversity of young people in silence for a few moments.

"Where were the children off to this morning?" Lady Douglas broke the silence first.

"I believe Miss Fenton said Eltham Palace. Of course Bella must take her sketch pad!"

"So gratifying to see Virginia taking an interest in something other than the latest Minerva Press novel. We've tried to keep them from her, but somehow she will acquire them!"

"Quite! Young girls are romantical enough today without reading such tripe! Miss Fenton has proved to be an excellent choice for companion in this regard, for she has literary ambitions and insists that Bella read the classics."

The butler bowed in more guests calling on the duchess, thus ending the two ladies' tête-à-tête. Meanwhile, the subjects of their self-congratulatory conversation were in the duchess's second-best brougham, bowling through London's busy streets toward Fitzroy Square, the center of London's artistic community, and a part of London to which no gently bred young lady should be journeying. Moreover, they were going there to keep a rendezvous with one of the *ton*'s premier rakes!

"She is making good progress, don't you agree?" Harrison Curzon managed to control his impulse to smile triumphantly at Maillot as he showed off Isabella's latest efforts.

"Assuredly, the chit has ability," Maillot grudgingly admitted, "and has begun to improve her mastery of perspective."

"But?" Curzon knew Maillot too well to suppose he would leave any praise unleavened with criticism. It was what made him at the same time a valuable and a painful teacher.

"I very much fear her brushwork has deteriorated in these two weeks since accepting your tutelage."

Curzon turned to the two new paintings that Isabella was working on. "I had not noticed before. She is imitating my handling of paint, isn't she?"

"Regrettably, yes. It is one thing for you to dab it on in such a way, for you at least know the correct manner, though you do not choose to follow it."

"I have been experimenting," Curzon defended himself.

"Just so, and not entirely unsuccessfully, but the chit will ruin herself copying such an unusual style. She should first master classical techniques. Then, if she feels she must, she may experiment with her own style. Not yours!"

"Well, since her first choice of a tutor has an unreasoning prejudice against females—"

"Not unreasoning at all. Based upon a sound knowledge of the sex." Jean Maillot's mouth firmed.

"Perhaps you ought to set aside your prejudices for her. You cannot deny either her talent or her determination, at this point."

Maillot paced the studio, scowling, studying Isabella's early efforts, which were scattered about the room, sporting Curzon's charcoal emendations.

Curzon was silent. Maillot did not respond well to either coaxing or coercion. At last the artist faced his pupil and friend. "But how can you teach her with a veritable gaggle of females present? Don't they gabble and sigh and pace about?"

Resisting the temptation to draw attention to Maillot's pacing, a standard and distracting behavior of his, Curzon shook his head. "It is what I feared, too. But Miss Fenton is a budding poet. She sits quietly writing. As for Miss Douglas, unless I need her to look up at me, most of the time she reads novels, having apparently been deprived of all but improving works and sermons. And Bella is so immersed in her work a grenade could go off in the room and she wouldn't notice."

Maillot turned back to the current work in progress, a study of the Rye House Gateway, in Hertfordshire. "Perhaps I might just drop by the next time she is here, then. At least warn her about the problem."

"Excellent! I expect her within the hour." Curzon slapped Maillot on the back. He hadn't the least doubt that his friend would be unable to resist demonstrating correct brushwork to Isabella. Far from being unwilling to share his pupil, Harrison had a sincere concern that she not form any bad habits under his tutelage. He was aware that he still had much to learn himself.

Thus it was that, scarcely an hour later, Isabella found herself listening raptly to the lecture that Maillot launched into as soon as he entered the room. He illustrated his suggestions by taking up her brush and painting directly on her canvas.

Their two heads were close together, discussing precisely the amount of linseed oil she should use to thin her paint. A few feet away Virginia posed in her drape of pale green satin while Harrison put the finishing touches on her portrait. Nearby, on another easel, stood a very large canvas with a preliminary sketch on it. Curzon had decided to paint Bella as if she were painting Virginia, and add it to his series of canvases depicting the activities of young women of various social classes.

At the table across the room Miss Fenton's lips were moving silently as she read over her morning's production. It was a peaceful scene until the Dowager Duchess of Carminster charged in on them.

Chapter Six

Harrison turned at the sound of someone entering the room. He recognized the elegant gray-haired woman immediately, though he had seldom exchanged words with her. Everyone in the *ton* knew that tall, imposing female who wore her many years so gracefully. The dowager stood with both hands on her cane, surveying the room's occupants.

At her elbow stood the footman who had accompanied her up the stairs. Behind her stood Lady Douglas. It was she who spoke first, her voice shrill.

"What is the meaning of this," she demanded, stepping around the duchess. "Virginia, what are you doing?"

Virginia scrambled down from the dais on which she had been seated, trailing the length of pale green satin behind her. "I can explain, Mama."

"You had best do so at once." Lady Douglas glared at Mr. Curzon. "What can you be about, sir, clandestinely shutting yourself up with my daughter in this seedy part of town?"

Bella left her canvas to stand by Curzon's side. "He is painting Ginny's portrait, Lady Douglas. It was to be a surprise for your wedding anniversary."

Virginia's mother moved so that she could see the canvas and drew in her breath sharply. "Why . . . why so he is. Do look, Your Grace; it is exquisite."

The dowager stalked to the canvas. "Hmmph!" She surveyed the preliminary sketches of Bella and Virginia on the larger canvas, then slowly made her way to the painting her granddaughter had been working on. She glared at Maillot, who stood in front of it with brush in hand. He hadn't moved since she entered the room. Her shrewd blue eyes widened with recognition of the painting. "Rye House Gateway," she snapped. "How does it happen that you are copying my granddaughter's painting, sir?"

Maillot exploded. "Copying? Jean Maillot, copying? Copying from a little chit of a girl! You are an idiot, madam."

"Don't you call my grandmother an idiot!" Bella stormed to the duchess's defense.

"So! *You* are Jean Maillot. When did you begin sneaking around to take pupils, sir? Particularly innocent young girls without the permission of their guardians! You refused to come to my home to teach her, yet here she is in your studio. It is a great impertinence. I shall see that you are ruined for this. No one in England will ever purchase a painting of yours again when I am though with you."

"No, Grandmama! Mr. Maillot was not—"

"Sneaking! I'll have you know I do not sneak, madam. Nor do I teach females, especially females of your class." Maillot shook his fist at Curzon. "You see, Harry. You see why I avoid these creatures! My prospects destroyed, on the whim of a silly chit!"

Harrison closed the distance between himself and the duchess. "This is my studio, Your Grace. Mr. Maillot is blameless in this affair."

"Affair! My baby ruined!" Lady Douglas began to cry.

"Ruined. Mama! No! Do not say so." Virginia began to weep as well.

"Your Grace," Mary Fenton began, "I can explain . . ."

"That isn't what he meant, Lady Douglas." Bella stamped her foot angrily. "There is no affair, and no sneaking around, either. Mr. Maillot came up here not five minutes ago to see Mr. Curzon. I prevailed upon him to critique my painting."

The duchess rapped her cane sharply on the floor. "No

sneaking around? Then please be so good as to explain what you are doing here instead of at Eltham Palace?"

Bella opened her mouth for an instant, then closed it.

"Ha! Can't answer me, can you, missy. Go down to our carriage, at once, Isabella Eardley. I will deal with you later. Miss Fenton, you are discharged. Mr. Maillot, you had best begin packing. I think America beckons. And as for you, Harrison Curzon, I shall be speaking with your father—"

"No!" Bella charged up to her grandmother. Hands on hips, she glared at the dowager. In spite of the difference in their height, she seemed quite as imposing as the *grande dame*. "You listen to me, before you begin ruining lives with the same enthusiasm as my father."

"And for the same reason, Bella. Because of your pranks."

"Yes, Grandmama, because of *my* pranks. All of these people are blameless. It was all my idea, and my doing, and only I should be punished."

"I don't doubt you started this disaster, but you are the youngest person in the room. Older, wiser heads should have exercised more judgment. Go to the carriage."

"I won't! You must listen to me."

The duchess motioned to the footman. "Rogers, escort my granddaughter to the carriage, if you please, and see that she remains there."

Curzon stepped between the footman and Bella, who looked fully capable of scratching the servant's eyes out. "Not just yet, my man. Your Grace, I think you and Lady Douglas should be seated and listen to our explanations. I have always heard that you were a stickler for propriety, but I had not heard that you were unfair."

The duchess looked from Curzon's piercing ice blue eyes to the stubborn set of her granddaughter's body. A glance at the footman told her the man lacked the courage to confront Curzon. "How dare you intimidate my servant. You shall answer for this!"

"I am sure I will, but first I ask you to hear Miss Eardley out." He bowed formally and motioned toward the group of chairs around the table. "Won't you please be seated, ladies?"

Frigidly erect, the duchess sat on the very edge of her seat. Lady Douglas sat on another, dabbing at her eyes with a lacy handkerchief.

Isabella insisted on telling the story, and Curzon listened with admiration as she wove a tale that placed all of the blame on herself. "Virginia wanted to give her parents a portrait, but she couldn't afford an established painter. She had met Mr. Curzon through her cousin, and learned on her drive with him in the park that he was an artist. He showed her some of his paintings at Somerset House. As soon as I heard about it, I went there and viewed them. They were exquisite.

"Since she had already expressed a wish for me to paint her portrait, I suggested that she ask him instead. I talked Mary into chaperoning us. Mr. Curzon somewhat reluctantly agreed to do it. Mr. Maillot, as I said, only stopped in this morning by accident."

"It won't wash, Bella. You have a canvas in progress here, a smock to cover your clothes, and you have been bribing the second coachman not to tell where he has been taking you. If some urchins had not pelted the carriage with garbage yesterday, alerting Mitchell that Joshua had taken you somewhere he should not, it would never have occurred to me to suspect you."

Bella pulled her full lower lip into her mouth for an instant. "The secrecy was to prevent Virginia's mother from learning about the anniversary surprise. I didn't know whether you would agree or not, so I thought it better not to say anything. Also, Mr. Curzon wished to keep his studio private. When he learned that I was an aspiring artist, Mr. Curzon agreed to offer me some hints. I decided to use my time while waiting for him to paint Virginia's portrait to have another try at painting Braughing, following Mr. Curzon's suggestions."

The duchess looked from Bella to Virginia to Curzon. "Is this tale true, Virginia?"

Ginny nodded her head desperately. "It was all very innocent. I have been posing for two weeks. As you can see, the painting is beautiful. Don't you think it is, Mama? And what is the harm of Bella improving her art skills in the meantime, Your Grace?"

"The harm is that for two weeks the people responsible for your safety did not know where you were. Instead of studying architecture, you have been involved in a most improper situation—"

"How was it improper, Lady Douglas?" By-passing the implacable duchess, Curzon smiled ingratiatingly at Virginia's mother. "Miss Fenton was here to chaperone us. There was never an instant that I was alone with either girl."

Lady Douglas looked appealingly at the duchess. "It doesn't seem so very bad at that."

The dowager straightened. "Perhaps you can excuse Virginia's behavior. But my granddaughter has deceived me with the connivance of her governess. She has been in the clutches of a notorious rake. Very well, Maillot. You may go. I accept that you have had no improper role here." She waved an imperious hand in dismissal of the artist.

Maillot bowed angrily and stalked from the room without further ado.

"I cannot say the same for you, Mr. Curzon. You knew my granddaughter had no permission to be here."

Curzon nodded. "She might have sought it, were it not for your unreasonable stance on her studies."

The duchess stiffened. "What right have you to criticize me!"

"The right of a fellow artist who recognizes extraordinary talent when he sees it. Instead of scolding her, you should nurture her ability."

The duchess snapped, "I have done so. I engaged Mr. Morgan—"

"A dauber, ma'am. Your granddaughter could have taught *him* to his benefit. He is only fit to turn out lady-painters. Miss Eardley is a true artist."

"My granddaughter is also a lady, sir. Or at least I hope one day to make a lady of her." The duchess stood. "Come, Bella. We will discuss your behavior in private."

Isabella determinedly linked her arm with Mary Fenton's. "Come, Mary."

"I don't think her Grace wishes me to do so."

"You shan't turn her off, Grandmama!"

"We will discuss it later. Come along, Miss Fenton. Aramintha?"

Virginia's mother stepped over to view the painting of Virginia once more. "It is truly beautiful, Mr. Curzon. Thomas Lawrence could not do better." Curzon bowed silently, but his handsome face flushed with pleasure at this encomium.

"Then you are pleased, Mama? Do say you will not forbid Mr. Curzon to call on me?"

Lady Douglas frowned. "Like the duchess, I cannot like the element of deception involved here. Not in seeking to surprise me. I know you meant well there. But to place yourself in the hands of such a gentleman . . ."

Curzon stiffened. His eyes began to glitter dangerously as he listened to mother and daughter argue.

"You let him take me for a drive. I thought—"

"Ginny, there is a world of difference in driving in an open carriage in the park and coming to such an unfashionable part of town and shutting yourself up with Mr. Curzon . . ." Lady Douglas took note of Curzon's increasingly offended expression. " . . . or any other man, for that matter. You will have to be disciplined in some way. As for seeing Mr. Curzon again, it is something I must consider."

She nodded to Harrison. "I bid you good day, sir."

She took Virginia's arm and half dragged the reluctant girl from the room. At the head of the stairs she turned back. "May we take the painting, Mr. Curzon?"

"It is not quite finished, ma'am. I can complete it within a day or two, but then it must dry. I will bring it to you in a couple of weeks. I hope and believe that you will receive me then."

"Ummmm." Lady Douglas eyed him consideringly. "We will see."

"Grandmama, please don't let Mary go without a reference. It is all my fault, I tell you. I persuaded her much against her better judgment. You could not be so unfair."

"It is not unfair to dismiss a servant who has behaved in such a duplicitous way when entrusted with a young girl's safety," the duchess responded firmly. "If you do not know what a London mob is capable of, she does. She had no business letting you go into that part of town. I will pay her what I owe her to this day. Nothing more, and I wish to hear no more from you on this head."

Bella worried at her bottom lip. "And Joshua?"

"Another faithless servant. He will also be discharged."

"I won't allow it! I shall pay them out of my allowance!"

"As of today, you will have no allowance save some pin money, and you will account to me in detail for every farthing of that!"

"You can't do that! It is my money, left me by my grandfather Eardley," Bella stormed.

The duchess stood up. "Enough. Go to your room and begin packing, missy."

"P-packing? Where . . ."

"I am returning you to your parents. You are too much for me to deal with. My age begins to weigh upon me at times like this." And indeed, the duchess did look every one of her eighty-one years at this minute, a fact that smote at Bella's heart.

She launched herself across the room to kneel at her grandmother's feet. "No, Grandmama! I am so sorry. I have been very wicked. I truly did not mean to trouble you." She lifted her hands prayerfully. "Never say I must return to Papa. He will make me wed old Lord Nielson."

"Who will feel much, much older after having you to wife for a week, I make no doubt. Get up, child! No more of these dramatics. They are exhausting me."

"Please say you will let me stay. I will behave myself. You'll see. I'll be a paragon of propriety."

"Ha!" The duchess looked down into the tear-streaked face turned up to hers. "I cannot deal with these excesses of emotion. Calm yourself, or leave me immediately."

Wiping her eyes with the palms of her hands, Bella retreated to her chair. The duchess lowered herself wearily onto the sofa where she had been sitting. She studied her granddaughter somberly. The clock on the mantel was the only sound in the room as Bella waited, hardly daring to breathe.

"I can see that it won't do to leave you in the care of others. First you take up Miss Henderson's radical ideas, then you suborn Miss Fenton. If you are to stay here, in future you will be answerable to me. You will accompany me everywhere and receive with me when I am at home."

Bella wanted to argue this dire sentence, but bit her lip and remained silent.

"You will account to me for every minute of your time, and if you are ever not where you are supposed to be, I will have Betty pack your things and you will be on your way back to Hertfordshire within the hour, no matter whether it be day or night. Is that understood?"

Bella nodded mutely.

"Let me hear your word on it."

"I will do just as you ask, Grandmother. Not merely because you threaten to send me home, either. I see how much of a trial I have been to you, and I am truly sorry."

"Hmmmph." The dowager shook her head. "You will pardon me if I suspect you of Spanish coin. You must prove yourself to me, missy."

Bella's head drooped. "Yes, Grandmama. I understand."

"And I forbid you to paint anymore."

Bella moaned. "Must you?"

The dowager grimaced. "At least until I am quite sure you have mended your ways. Instead, we will begin working on refining your deportment and dancing skills. Your piano work is excellent, but you must practice each day, for you will be expected to exhibit your accomplishments. And we can continue building your wardrobe in preparation for the season."

Bella drew in a deep, shuddering breath. *Not to be able to paint! How will I endure it?* Still, she must avoid returning to her father's ambitious clutches at all costs. "Very well, Grandmama. I shall prepare myself to be a credit to you."

The dowager stood. "Good. I am going to rest for a while. Be so good as to go to your room and remain there until dinner. We dine with the Grimwolds this evening."

The Grimwolds! They are every bit as grim as their name, Bella thought as she climbed the stairs to her room. But there was no rebellion in her heart. She must succeed in remaining with her grandmother at all costs.

As Bella dragged herself slowly to her room, she saw a footman bearing a trunk, followed by Mary Fenton. "Oh,

Mary." She rushed up to her companion and threw her arms around her. "I am so sorry! What will you do? Where will you go?"

"Back to Mrs. Parminter's rooms for ladies, I expect. Though she will have some sharp questions for me about why I have left my employment."

"I had intended to continue your salary if you came to any harm because of me, but Grandmama is going to cut off my allowance." Bella wrung her hands. "I must help you somehow."

"I shall contrive, Bella—"

"I know something I can do. Come with me." Isabella grabbed Miss Fenton's hand.

"No, Bella. No use making your grandmother any angrier than she already is. She told me to leave immediately."

"She's gone to bed. Come. There is something I must give you." Bella half pulled her governess into her room. Crossing to her jewelry box, she opened it and lifted out the top compartment. Taking out a heavy purse, she turned and held it out to Miss Fenton.

"This is the rest of my quarter's allowance. You must find Joshua, the coachman, and give him ten guineas. He's been let go, too, because of me. The rest is yours. And I shall write you a reference and send it along to you at Mrs. Parminter's."

"A reference? I suppose you would forge the duchess's signature, Bella? I think not."

Bella dimpled. "No, that would be too obvious. Your reference shall be from a matron, expressing gratitude for your care of her three children before she departed for the Canadian provinces."

Mary grinned at her former charge. "You are a complete hand, Bella. But I don't think I will accept. My career until now has been blameless. I shrink from any further deception. Besides, with any luck at all I won't need that reference."

"You have an idea. Tell me, tell me!"

Mary looked behind them to be sure no one was listening at the door. "Lady Langley has asked me if I would consider working for her when your season is over and you are safely married. She is finding it difficult to keep up with all of her duties with a new baby to care for. I would be part personal secretary and part editorial assistant. And in my spare time I can write poetry!"

"That is of all things wonderful." Bella's enthusiasm was genuine. She felt a great weight of guilt lift from her shoulders. "This purse will help you get by until then." Bella thrust it into Mary's hands.

Mary accepted it reluctantly. "Very well, Bella, I will take it and see that Joshua receives his share. But I am hoping when Lady Langley learns I am at leisure, she will ask me to begin working for her right away."

Bella hugged Mary. "I expect great things from you. You'll see. One day historians will look back on us and write of England's first great female poet and first great female landscape artist!"

"Ah, Bella." Mary's hands cupped Isabella's cheeks tenderly. "I do hope both of us don't get our wings singed, trying to fly so high."

Chapter Seven

"Damn you, Curzon! I'll tear you limb from limb."

"A good evening to you, too, Gilbert. Your visit is not entirely unexpected." Harrison Curzon dismissed his valet with a toss of his head and completed an elaborate arrangement of his neckcloth with smooth expertise.

"I'll vow you did. Shall it swords or pistols, you despoiler of innocence?"

Curzon surveyed Lord Threlbourne in the mirror. His face was as red as his hair, and his green eyes, so like Virginia's, were flashing with anger. "Such histrionics. Exactly what did they tell you, Gil?"

"Don't 'Gil' me! You're no friend of mine."

"I think you are in love with your cousin," Harrison drawled as he turned slowly, coolly flexing his arms to straighten his cuffs as he did so.

"That is nothing to the point."

"I think it is, for I very much suspect she returns your regard."

Diverted from his vengeful intentions, Gilbert put his hand to the back of his neck and shook his head ruefully. "You're fair and far out there. She will have none of me."

"For your information, Gilbert, I have been contemplating marrying your lovely cousin, but second thoughts assail me each time she mentions you. Shall I tell you my assessment of her feelings?"

"After you tell me your choice of seconds and weapons."

"Rot. I won't meet you. Virginia has taken no harm from me. We were fully chaperoned by Miss Eardley's governess on every occasion but the first. Despite the duchess's suspicions, Miss Fenton was quite concerned for the proprieties."

"Which you ignored, at least once, by your own admission."

"Only to the extent of showing my studio to her and Isabella. You should thank me for keeping that naughty pair out of other mischief. Let me tell you of their first visit."

After Curzon had put him in possession of the facts, Gilbert groaned. "Hoydens, both of them. I'm not surprised, though. When she was a child, Ginny was up to every rig and row. She just doesn't seem to understand as yet the kind of dangers a young girl can get herself into."

"Such as landing in the clutches of a rake like me?"

"Precisely!"

"If I am such an unconscionable rake, how does it happen that both she and Miss Eardley have emerged from the experience with virtue intact?"

"Did they?" Curzon could see the aching vulnerability behind Gilbert's fierce demand.

"Word of honor. Gil, you know innocent females have never been in my line. Even my bits of muslin have been experienced. Except in a wife, I see virginity as a drawback, not a desirable trait, in a woman. Now come downstairs with me, and let's crack a bottle of brandy together while we decide how to determine the state of Miss Douglas's affections."

Gilbert allowed himself to be escorted out of Curzon's bedchamber and downstairs, where he gloomily took a seat and the proffered glass of French brandy.

"Can't think why you believe Virginia might have anything other than cousinly affection for me," he sighed as he contemplated the amber liquid. "She's done naught but defy her family's attempts to marry us since first she heard of the scheme."

"Does she know how you feel about her?"

Gilbert shook his head. "Have some pride, y'know. Her rejection was so absolute, so vociferous, I had no wish to expose my heart to her cutting little tongue. Partly her father's fault, I know. He handled her all wrong. She is too hot to hand to try to command into marriage. I wanted her to have a season, meet other men. Then I meant to court her myself."

"Hmmm. That explains why you encouraged Lady Douglas to receive me." Curzon swished his brandy around and then tossed it back. "I think all Miss Virginia Douglas requires is some sign of your affection."

Gilbert shook his head despairingly. "That would send her scampering in the other direction. Besides, she thinks me boring and stuffy."

"Ironic, isn't it, for you are generally accredited as a nonesuch by those in the know. Could her attitude be caused by the fact that you both preach and practice propriety with her? My reading of her character is that she would like you a deal better if you cut a bit of a dash around her, as you are certainly capable of doing."

A flicker of hope lightened Gilbert's expression. "You may be right. We were always getting into mischief together as children, but I've felt so protective of her since she became a young woman."

"That's right. You've not let her see the real you. Incidentally, I think letting her see you squiring Delilah Blessington was a good idea."

Gilbert leaned forward, eyes wide. "What did she say? Was she jealous?"

"She pronounced her a coming female, likely to live up to her name."

A wide grin spread over Gilbert's face. "Then it was having some effect. But I'm in danger there. Delilah has missed two seasons because of deaths in her family. Her parents are terrified she'll remain on the shelf. Many more invitations to drive in the park, and I'll be well on my way to being leg-shackled."

"Quite a predicament. Select another, less eager, female."

"In case you haven't noticed, town is very thin of company just now." Gilbert's mouth slanted in a wry smile.

"How about Miss Eardley?"

"Huh! She is a complete hoyden, if not worse. Far from courting her, I wish to keep Virginia from being contaminated by further contact with her."

"That is very harsh. She is just a high-spirited miss like Virginia."

"Dressing as a boy, declaring her intention to be a professional artist! The very idea of a *ton* female with aspirations to artistic fame!"

"Yes, it is quite as ridiculous as a gentleman taking his art seriously, isn't it?" Curzon stared moodily into the fire. *No one but I can understand Isabella. Come to that, no one but she can understand me.*

"Nevertheless, she is a very pretty young female whose family mean to find her a husband. They'd welcome your invitations, and unless I miss my guess, Virginia would soon show green in more than those pretty eyes. I hope I am wrong, of course. If she shows herself indifferent to you, I mean to have her myself."

Gilbert shook his head. "I'll do what I must to prevent that."

"Why? I won't be a bad husband to her. Indeed, I shall cherish her. She is a magnificent creature with that red-gold hair, that ravishing coloring!"

Gilbert's expression was grim. "Your feelings are all bound up in her beauty. I loved her when her face was covered with freckles, and I'll love her when she is gray and wrinkled. Can you honestly say that when she is no longer young and beautiful you will find anything about her to keep you at her side?"

Curzon swung his gaze away from the fire and frowned uncomfortably at the younger man's challenge. "I don't know. Only time would tell."

"Here is an invitation you may enjoy, Bella." The Dowager Duchess of Carminster held up a sheet of expensive writing paper. "The Blessingtons are giving a dinner, to be followed by dancing. Not a ball, precisely, for as Mrs. Blessington writes, there are too few in town to make a creditable ball, but a dancing party. Their daughter Delilah is older than you, but has been kept from a season by a series of deaths in her family.

The duchess scrutinized her granddaughter's face for any signs of pleasure. The child had been as well-behaved as anyone could wish the last two weeks, but there was no joy in her. Before, she had seemed to bounce as she walked, and sparkle as she talked, but since that day she had been caught out in her pranks, she had grown more and more subdued. Even the eligible Lord Threlbourne's calls had brought no animation to her. She accepted his invitations politely, but her demeanor with him was uncharacteristically passive.

I suppose I shall have to let her return to painting, the duchess thought. *Something has gone out of her since I shut up her studio.*

"That's lovely, Grandmama," Bella said without conviction. "What shall I wear?"

The only thing Bella had shown any enthusiasm about since the duchess had taken her in hand had been her wardrobe. She had thrown herself into the study of fashion, and even made suggestions on the design of her gowns, which Madame de Coursey had readily accepted, declaring that the young woman understood her own type very well.

When the duchess had demurred at Bella's insistence on some color in her gowns, rather than the virginal white that society thought so delightful for a young lady in her first season, Madame de Coursey had upheld Bella's choice. "She cannot wear the pure white, Your Grace. She must have at the least ivory, else her complexion will look pasty. There must always be some color near her face, as well. She will be *ravissement* in pale gold, or this daffodil yellow.

"She is petite, yet very feminine. Her challenge will be to make the gentlemen see her as a woman, not a child. Color will assist her. Also, I would suggest, Your Grace, that her evening gowns must show a lower décolletage than most such young misses wear. She has the very pretty bosom. With the right sort of gown, the gentlemen cannot miss seeing that she is a woman grown." The modiste had twitched draped fabric this way and that while she and Isabella chattered away. They ended by convincing the dowager that some color in Isabella's wardrobe would be acceptable for a woman so small and blond.

"I think I would look well in aqua, too," Bella had said. "And I know I wear true blue tones well, for my riding habit is blue." Relieved to see the child taking an interest in something practical for a change, the duchess had allowed Bella to choose her own clothes.

Remembering that conversation, the duchess suggested, "This party would be a good occasion to wear your pale aqua gauze gown."

She was rewarded by the appearance of some animation to her granddaughter's features. "That is my favorite," Bella said. "Shall I wear flowers in my hair?"

She will be all right once she begins going about in society, the duchess reassured herself. *She will soon forget this obsession with painting.*

* * *

"Your cousin is in looks tonight."

Lord Threlbourne drew in his breath as he turned in the direction of Harrison Curzon's avid gaze. "She looks like a breath of spring on this chilly May evening!" Gilbert abandoned Harrison to greet his cousin. Harry observed with interest the manner in which Virginia responded to this greeting. Hope flared as he observed the exquisite redhead nod coolly to her cousin before turning to speak to another acquaintance.

"Apparently you haven't succeeded in making her jealous by squiring Isabella Eardley," he said as Threlbourne retreated to the pillar the two had been holding up together moments earlier.

Gilbert shook his head mournfully. "She hasn't so much as turned a hair, though she saw me driving her in the park twice."

"And how does the fair Isabella?" Curzon was genuinely curious. He had been unable to gather any intelligence of the dynamic little blonde's situation since the debacle in his studio. He hadn't even bothered to attempt calling on her, given the dowager's ill-concealed dislike for him. Inquiries of Virginia were fruitless. He had been permitted to call on her, but her mother had decided that Isabella was a bad influence, and kept the two apart.

Gilbert considered the question a moment. "She is a colorless little thing with very little conversation. Nor does she have the least idea how to draw a man out. Shows no interest in my cattle, nor in my driving skill. Was totally unimpressed that I beat Prinny's time for driving from London to Brighton. Really, I do not think she has any interest in me at all, which is to the good as far as that goes, for I needn't fear she'll try to leg-shackle me as Delilah Blessington would."

"Colorless? 'Tis the last word I'd have chosen to describe her. Ah, speak of the devil, or angel, for such she looks tonight!" Curzon gestured with his head toward the door to the salon, where the Blessingtons were informally welcoming their guests.

I wonder if she is still painting? Have they hired another teacher for her? Curzon found the questions crowding his mind as he watched Bella, very prettily gowned in aqua gauze, greet her host and hostess. He waited until the duchess had been distracted by a matronly woman in a high turban, and then approached Isabella.

"Miss Eardley," he greeted her softly. She turned slowly and lifted dull eyes to his. But immediately upon seeing who had spoken to her, she changed. Her smile brought several enchanting dimples into play. Her bright blue eyes gleamed.

"Mr. Curzon! How very good to see you here." She looked uneasily at her grandmother. Taking the hint, he drew her several feet away, with a tall Chinese vase between them and the dowager.

"You look ravishing," he told her quite sincerely. Of course he had remarked her prettiness before, but somehow he had missed noticing what a very desirable female she was.

She waved her hand dismissively. It was not compliments she hungered for. "Have you kept working on the painting of Virginia and me? I expect it must be very difficult without your subjects around."

"It is not a problem with Ginny, for I still have her other portrait to guide me. But your coloring has eluded me." He moved her closer to a candle branch. "I confess I had not studied you carefully before."

She giggled. "No, you had eyes only for Virginia, and why not. She is a beauty. Doesn't she look marvelous tonight? I had not thought she could wear white so well."

Curzon turned in the direction she was looking. Virginia was now on Lord Threlbourne's arm; her mother was on his other side.

"Not a blank white, though. Well chosen for her," Curzon mused after running a knowledgeable eye over Virginia. "More of an oyster white."

He turned back to Isabella. "I had not remembered your eyes being that precise color of blue. More of an aquamarine."

"It is this dress, I expect." Bella spread the skirt of her gown, fingering the sheer fabric with pleasure.

"But tell me, what would you use to convey your skin tones? You are very fair, but not pink and white like most blondes."

Her eyes twinkled with glee at being consulted by such an outstanding artist. "I am surprised you don't know. Haven't you ever done a self-portrait?"

He lifted an inquisitive eye. "Of course."

"We have much the same coloring. Oh, you are much darker, of course, from exposure to the sun. But we both have a golden cast to our skin. Try a touch of burnt sienna." She studied his face dispassionately. "I have been trying to remember just what shade your eyes are. Now I see they have a great many white flecks in them, which is why they are so light and seem to glitter. At first I thought them cold, but tonight they look quite warm. Your pupils are very large tonight."

"That is because I am looking at you. Don't you know that desire enlarges the pupils?" He gave her his most rakish look.

Isabella didn't pink up at all. "It is because you are discussing painting. I am starved for such a conversation."

"As am I," Curzon admitted.

"But no one tells you that you can't paint." Bella looked away, clenching her jaws.

"Has that been your fate?"

"My grandmother threatened to send me home if I didn't behave myself, and my punishment is not to paint or draw."

Curzon felt his fists clench. "That is an inhuman sentence."

She lifted grateful eyes to his. "No one but you would understand that." Warmth filled Bella, warmth and a sudden sense of safe harbor. She felt an urge to draw nearer to him and have him gather her into his strong arms.

Curzon experienced a sudden sensation of drowning as he looked into Isabella's eyes. For a few moments the room and its occupants faded, and there were only the two of them. But a familiar voice brought them both back to their senses.

"Isabella! It is so wonderful to see you." They both turned to find Virginia eagerly surveying her friend. "That gown is marvelous!"

Curzon turned to Threlbourne as the two young women renewed their acquaintance. "Are you making any progress?"

"Possibly." Gilbert rocked back on his heels. "At least, Virginia had heard of the Brighton venture and was most impressed."

"Who was not? The betting was heavily in your favor, of course."

"Did you lose on me?" Gilbert's eyes glinted sardonically.

"By no means. Know better than to bet against a whip of your ability."

Virginia turned at that. "Oh, you've heard of his accomplishment, then. How I wish I had seen it." She glanced up at her cousin, face flushed with pleasure.

Curzon scowled as he looked from one redhead to the other. *Is this love, or merely hero worship? It is time I found out exactly where matters stand with this minx*, he thought. For some reason he wasn't terribly interested in the outcome this evening. He glanced at Isabella, who was paying no attention to Gilbert. Her eyes were on him, and there was a look in them he could not quite interpret.

Surely not desire? A few moments ago she had either ignored or totally misunderstood his flirtatious manner. *She is but a baby.* He fought down the unexpected rush of awareness of Isabella. It was Virginia he wanted to marry; he had no business lusting after her young friend.

They were interrupted by their hostess, who had a gentleman in tow. She looked like a hunter who has just bagged a particularly fine grouse. "Miss Douglas, Miss Eardley, the Duke of Winkham has requested that I present him to you."

"*Enchanté,*" Winkham murmured over each young girl's hand, but his eyes quickly turned in undisguised admiration to Isabella.

"You here, Winky?" Gilbert drawled.

"How did you learn my school name, Threlbourne? Thought I'd outgrown it forever." Winkham did not look particularly displeased, however. "How am I to maintain my dignity before these beautiful young ladies?"

Curzon studied the Duke of Winkham curiously. Some seven years his senior, the duke was almost an unknown among the *ton*. Rumor had it that his mother had kept him firmly under her thumb until her death a little more than a year ago. A short, stocky man, the duke looked as if he could benefit from a trip to a good tailor.

He stood an inch or two shorter than Virginia, which perhaps explained his lack of interest in her. He had eyes only for the petite blonde. Curzon glanced at Bella, wondering what she thought of the duke. She was listening politely to his gallantries, her eyes studying him with avid interest. Doubtless Winkham thought she was taken with him, but Curzon choked back a chuckle, for he could almost hear her thinking, "Umber, not sienna, for the hair."

He turned his attention to Virginia, who was chatting

with their hostess. He must make a plan to get her to himself for an important tête-à-tête, and soon. His father was hoping he would bring home a prospective bride before the end of the season.

Late that night, Isabella turned this way and that in front of her dressing mirror. She was stark naked. On her dresser rested a drawing pad with a sketch of herself in the nude. She referred to her reflection in the mirror and then corrected a line on the drawing. When she was finally satisfied with the results, she turned back to run her hands over her body.

The mystery of touch had always intrigued her. Of course, her very strict nanny had forbidden her to touch herself anywhere but on her face and arms. But Bella was not the sort to adhere to rules she didn't agree with. She was familiar with her body and its various responses to her own touch. But for some odd reason, tonight she found herself wondering how it would feel when touched by a man, in the way that a lover would touch a woman.

The duke had been very interested in her tonight. Her grandmother had been in alt over it. She tried to imagine Winkham touching her so, and so. Gilbert? Harrison? At the thought of the blond giant bending to caress her, she felt a thrill rush through her. Her response did not surprise her. She had been aware of Harrison Curzon as a man and herself as a woman since the day she had met him. Just thinking of him as he had appeared the day of her first lesson, his muscular back straining against the cloth of his shirt as he stretched mightily, his strong arms bared, made her warm all over. Tonight that awareness of him had intensified, fight it though she might.

A profitless awareness, she reminded herself. *He is courting Virginia. He was but amusing himself by flirting with me tonight.* Reminding herself that she did not want to be courted by anyone, because she didn't want to marry, didn't seem to help. She was haunted by curly blond hair that seemed to entice her to run her hands through it, and ice blue eyes that were capable of looks that could melt. *Virginia is a very fortunate young woman*, she acknowledged to herself. Sadly, she turned from her reflection. She struggled into her soft muslin nightrail and blew out her candle. In the darkness, she could pretend . . .

Chapter Eight

While Isabella was sketching her reflection in her bedroom mirror, Harrison Curzon was seeking release from his tension over a *rouge et noir* table at Brooks's. Luck was with him. He was scooping up a huge pile of chips when he became aware of the Duke of Winkham at his elbow.

"D'ya have any system, old man?" the duke asked, admiration shining in his eyes.

Curzon smiled ruefully. "I seem to do best at the tables when I am at *point non plus* in my *affaires d'amour*." He straightened and started to walk away, observing as he did so, "I'd have a care, Winkham. Play is deep here."

Instead of taking Curzon's place at the table, the duke followed him. "Join me for a drink? I'd frankly appreciate the advice of such a knowing man about town as yourself."

Curzon was little inclined to nurture a friendship with the Duke of Winkham, a man his senior in years but much his junior in experience. However, he had even less desire to return to his lonely rooms at the early hour of two A.M. He nodded his agreement. For the next hour, Winkham pumped him for information on everything from his choice of bootmaker to his manner of tying neckcloths.

"I couldn't help but notice that your style is unique. That is, you did tie your cravat off-center on purpose, did you not?"

Curzon was sure the other man meant to flatter him with his blatant admiration, but he suddenly felt a little foolish for his carefully cultivated appearance. He knew he was generally admired for his dashing interpretations of current fashions, but did not care to be thought a dandy.

He shook his head, not quite in denial, more in self-mockery. "Actually, I am just a bit eccentric."

"I don't believe a word of it. Too cleverly done. I don't suppose you'd tell me how . . . ?"

"You must leave me some secrets, Your Grace."

"Oh, call me Winky. Everyone does. I wonder if you'd advise me on the purchase of some cattle? I heard that, fine a whip as Threlbourne is, he can't compare to you."

Curzon shook his head. "Not so. Gil is the best there is."

Winkham laughed and shook his finger at Harry. "I heard that you beat all comers in a famous race near Salisbury."

"I had the better team." Tiring of so much hero worship, Curzon stood. "Think I'll call it a night."

The duke stood too. "I expect you are going to call on one of your ladybirds. How many do you have in keeping this year?"

Curzon frowned. "Gossip certainly reaches deep into the hinterland. One would hardly guess you've been buried in the country."

"Arnold Lanscombe is a friend of mine. He's filled me in on things even the *Gazette* won't print. Know you had not one, not two, but three of the most beautiful actresses in London in keeping at one time."

Harry lifted and rotated his shoulders. "Don't remind me of it. I was but one-and-twenty then, an unlicked cub hell-bent on committing every folly of youth."

Winkham wagged his head knowingly. "I suppose you'll tell me you haven't even one such in your pocket now."

"Yes, I will tell you that, for it's true. Looking about me for a wife, don't you know. Not the done thing to court decent young ladies while squiring a member of the muslin company about."

"Ah, I see how it is! Well, you can rely on me to keep your secret." The duke winked broadly at him.

Seeing no point in wasting any more effort undeceiving a man so determined to be deceived, Curzon bid Winkham a curt good evening and departed Brooks's into the rain-swept London night.

"Very lovely," Virginia agreed as Harrison pointed out an exotic white orchid to her. She was either unaware or unalarmed that her maid Betty and the curator of the Chelsea Physics Gardens, in response to a shiny guinea for each, had abandoned them to their own devices. Her enthusiasm for the outing had been very agreeable when he had proposed a visit to the greenhouse. Harrison had high hopes that she would respond as favorably to his proposal of marriage.

"You are more exotic, and far more lovely than that orchid," he declared, carrying her hand to his lips.

"Oh!" Her delicate complexion flushed peach. "You shouldn't . . . why, where is my maid?" A tiny flare of alarm in her voice caused him to release her hand. "We shouldn't be alone like this."

"But that is precisely why I brought you here. It is too cold for a drive in my curricle today. I could think of no other way to be private with you for a few minutes. I have lured you here to talk of our future, not from any particular love of botanical gardens."

"Our future?" She lifted alarmed green eyes to his.

He motioned her to a convenient bench. "Yes, Virginia. Surely you realize that I am considering offering for you. But before I do so, I wish to know how you feel about me."

"I . . . I . . ."

He frowned. Her inability to answer him spontaneously made his optimism of a few minutes before seem foolish. "From time to time I have felt that your real affection is for your cousin Gilbert. I have no wish to wed a woman who loves another."

Virginia swelled up indignantly. "I most certainly do not! I am fond of Gil, of course, but that is as far as it goes."

"Good. That still leaves in question how you feel about me."

"I am not sure how to answer you. I like you very well indeed, but . . . this is surely a most improper conversation, sir." She made as if to rise, but he stayed her by catching hold of her shoulders.

"Virginia, if I were to offer for you, your mother would be delighted. Your father would be less so, but he surely would not refuse me if you were willing. The question is simple. Are you willing?"

Virginia caught her breath. "I am not sure. Forgive me, I should know by now, I expect, but I have so little experience of men, other than Gil, of course."

He smiled. "I know that you are an innocent, which is what I expect of a bride." He studied her blushing face carefully. He did not want to make the same mistake with her he had done with Davida Gresham, by too forceful a wooing. "May I kiss you, Virginia?"

"Kiss me! Oh, I don't think . . ."

"Does the thought of kissing me disgust you?"

"Not at all, but it is highly improper."

"I think it would be more improper to marry without knowing whether the intimate side of our marriage would be agreeable for both of us."

"A kiss would tell us that?"

"It would give us a very good hint."

"Oh. Well, then . . ." She looked around them carefully to be sure they were unobserved, then turned her face up and closed her eyes.

Smiling at her slightly pursed lips, he bestowed a gentle kiss on them and then drew back.

"Well?"

"Oh, that was quite nice." She looked relieved.

"Good. Let's try something more intimate."

Bewildered but game, she held her face up again. He kissed her more intensely this time, closing his eyes to inhale her delicate lilac perfume. She was warm and sweet and responsive. Desire flared within Harrison. Forgetting his earlier resolution to proceed cautiously, he deepened the kiss, tracing her lips with his tongue. Virginia gasped in surprise. Taking her open mouth as an invitation, he thrust his tongue within, and crushed her to him. The kiss was long and deep and very arousing for him. But gradually he became aware that Virginia was struggling in his arms. He released her at once and she sprang away from him.

"I did not give you leave to maul me! How dare you, sir!" She jumped up and backed away from him. Before he could soothe her fears, his shoulder was seized by a strong hand.

"I warned you, Harrison Curzon!" He spun around and found himself nose to nose with Gilbert. "How dare you treat my cousin in that disgusting way, like one of your doxies!"

"Gilbert! Are you following me again?" Virginia's scolding of her cousin lacked conviction this time, and she hastened to place him between herself and Curzon.

"I promised your father I'd look out for you, and a good thing too." Gilbert motioned angrily to Curzon. "Step outside and we shall settle this."

"We'll settle it now." Curzon glanced behind Gilbert to see Isabella, the Duke of Winkham, and Delilah Blessington gaping at them. He grinned wickedly. "After all, I asked Virginia's permission, and she—"

At that instant Gilbert's fist slammed into his mouth. Curzon had seen the blow coming, had in fact provoked it, for he knew Gilbert would not want the others to hear that

Virginia had been a willing participant in that kiss. His head snapped back. He assumed a boxer's stance and lashed out, landing a glancing blow to the side of his opponent's head. Instantly, Gilbert repaid him with a strong left jab that knocked him off his feet.

"Oh, Gilbert, look what you have done to Mr. Curzon," Virginia breathed. Lying on the ground, Harrison ruefully noted that there was more of admiration than censure in her voice.

It was Isabella Eardley who knelt beside him, her voice anxious. "Are you very badly hurt?"

Harrison tested his jaw gingerly, wiggling it back and forth. "No teeth lost, jaw not broken. I believe I shall live. Are you satisfied, Gilbert."

"Not if you intend forcing your attentions on Virginia anymore."

Curzon looked up at Virginia, who stood transfixed at the ferocious look on her cousin's face. He glanced at the others. Winkham looked eager for the fight to continue. Delilah's eyes were wide with alarm. Isabella, too, was transfixed, but her eyes were on him. He saw in her face the genuine concern that had been lacking in Virginia's response. He had found out what he wanted to know.

He rose to his feet to begin dusting the gravel of the garden's pathways off his impeccably tailored jacket and trousers. "No, I think Virginia has made her preference clear. You have won the fair maiden, Gil. Best wishes."

Gilbert looked at Curzon's outstretched hand, then turned to his cousin. "Ginny? Do you feel this miscreant has been punished sufficiently."

"Please do not engage in any more vulgar brawling," she replied with a sniff. "You've milled him down once, that is quite enough." Tilting her head up, she marched past her cousin and took the duke's arm. "Is there room in your carriage for me? I think I would prefer not to ride with Mr. Curzon."

Bella had stood up when Curzon did. She reached up to touch his jaw. "Poor man. You are going to have a dreadful bruise there."

"Thank you for caring, Miss Eardley." Curzon took her small hand in his and kissed it gently.

"Come along, Bella," Winkham ordered, tugging on her arm. "Harrison Curzon is not such a weakling as to be undone by two blows."

Gilbert remained where he was as the others moved toward the entrance to the gardens. He eyed Curzon curiously. "Never knocked you down so easily in Gentleman Jackson's parlor, Harry."

"You weren't fighting for your true love then, Gil."

"Hmpf. You aren't fooling me. Dropped your guard on purpose." Gil shook his head. He turned to watch Virginia's stiff back as she marched away from them. "I think you may be right. She looked almost admiringly at me just then."

"Go along, then. Don't leave her to the duke."

Gilbert turned away, calling over his shoulder, "No fear. Winky has eyes for no one but Isabella. Think there's a match in the offing there."

I begin to think I shall have to let my father purchase me a bride after all, Curzon thought dispiritedly as he watched his beautiful redhead walk away. *I seem to have no sense at all when it comes to gently bred young ladies.* Yet he realized to his surprise that all he felt was a vague regret at the loss of Virginia.

"Well, Bertram, what brings you to town?" The dowager duchess greeted her son-in-law sourly.

"Must be here to dance the first dance with my beloved daughter at her ball, mustn't I?"

"You are unconvincing as a loving parent, Bertram." The duchess looked down on him from her advantageous height as if he were an insect.

"Aren't you going to offer me a seat?" Eardley demanded. With a sigh the duchess sat and indicated a chair to her son-in-law. "Please come to the point of this visit. I have calls to make."

He drew from his pocket a clipping from the *Gazette*. "I want to meet this 'Duke of W' who is said to be courting 'a certain blond niece of the Duke of C'."

"You pay far too much attention to the papers, Bertram. Vulgar gossip."

"Who is the Duke of W?" Bertram Eardley possessed a bulldoglike persistence. When he thrust his jaw out in that way, the duchess knew he would not be fobbed off.

"The Duke of Winkham. And yes, he is one of Bella's most frequent callers. I can't say how she feels about him."

"That is precisely why I am here, to be sure you don't let a lot of sentimental twaddle about her feelings keep her from making an outstanding match!" Eardley rubbed his hands together. "Winkham. Unexceptionable! More than that—outstanding!"

"I have already told you I won't see her forced into a match she despises. Now go back to Hertfordshire and tend your pigs, Bertram."

"So unwelcoming. Mean to stay in town. Mean to squire my daughter about, meet her friends, what?"

The duchess leaned forward and fixed him with her most repressive stare. "I can't think of anything more likely to scuttle her chances of a good match. You are trying to climb socially on her skirts, but your presence here will force upon her suitors the inescapable fact that you are not good *ton*. In fact, you are not *ton* at all! I curse my husband each time I think of Seraphina rotting in Hertfordshire with such as you."

Bertram Eardley jumped to his feet and stood over the duchess, hands balled into fists. "Watch your tongue, old woman, or I'll knock it down your throat."

"Sit down, sir!" The duchess thumped her cane against the floor vigorously. "Your impertinence is disgusting. Don't think to frighten me with your threats. Unlike poor Seraphina, I am not bound by law to let you beat me. I should like above all things to see you in Newgate for assaulting the person of a duchess!"

Eardley fell back before the venom in the duchess's expression. He sat, taking out a large kerchief to mop his suddenly damp brow.

"As I said, go back to Hertfordshire. I cannot guarantee that Isabella will wed a duke, but I, and I alone, can see that she marries into the *ton*."

Eardley put away his kerchief. A sly look came into his eyes. "I expect I will have to put up at the Pulteney."

"You mean to stay in spite of what I have said?"

"Seraphina has not been to London in years. Moreover, she is eager to see Isabella. She'd be disappointed if we turned right around and went back."

"Seraphina is here?" The duchess half stood, then sank back into her chair. "You've made her stay in the carriage, haven't you, odious man."

"Just wanted to be sure that *we* were welcome."

The duchess tried to stare him out of countenance, but Eardley crossed his arms and sat back in his chair, swinging his foot nonchalantly.

The duchess's furious glare gradually gave way to a thoughtful frown. "I have a bargain to propose to you, Bertram. You obviously haven't the least hesitation in using Seraphina as a pawn."

Eardley smiled. "Go on, dearest mother-in-law. I am listening."

The duchess picked up her cane again and put both hands on it, contemplating them as she thought. "I will give you house room here, if you will leave Seraphina with me when you return to Hertfordshire."

"Do you mean permanently?"

"Exactly."

Eardley shook his head, making his fat jowls shimmy. "Oh, no, I couldn't part with my beloved wife. Not for so paltry a thing as your brief, cold hospitality."

The duchess suppressed her fury at the man who had spitefully kept her daughter from her for over five years. "I had something a little more valuable to you in mind."

"Go on."

"I will not only give you house room here, but will sponsor you in the *ton*. Mind, you must agree to be guided by me in your choice of friends and your town manners. This is what you have wanted all of these years, after all."

Eardley eyed her suspiciously but it was as she said. This sort of entree into society was exactly what he wanted. "And you'll do your best to further the match with Winkham?"

The duchess inclined her head in agreement.

"Done."

Harrison Curzon sighed wearily as he pulled off his heavy, many-caped coat and hung it up. At least the porter had been here: the studio was warm. For May, the day was once again miserably cold and rainy. *But not as miserable as these interminable debates in the House of Commons*, he thought, shedding his suit coat and pulling his once-elaborate cravat from around his neck. This particular debate had been about Catholic emancipation, and had dragged on into the wee hours of the morning.

Instead of going home afterward, Curzon had decided to come to his studio and try to recover his sanity by painting for a few hours. He had little enough time to do so lately. His father had suggested that he begin attending the House of Commons. "Find out whether you like it or not. You have a fairly good idea of what the life of a country gentleman is. You may find politics more stimulating."

But Harrison did not find politics stimulating. He found it disgusting and boring and probably fruitless, for it seemed that no one ever changed his mind about anything as the result of the impassioned debates.

He consulted his watch, then the windows. *Five a.m. Not enough light to paint, right now. I'll just catch a nap for an hour or so.* Sighing deeply, he settled into the smooth leather of the sofa, which faced the fireplace, pillowing his head on his left arm.

"Mr. Curzon is expecting me," the cherubic blond page responded when challenged by the porter. He brandished a portfolio almost as large as he was. Grumbling, the porter waved him upstairs. Making sure the old man had retreated to the warmth of his quarters, the page bent toward the lock, a hair pin at the ready. Once inside, Bella set the portfolio against the wall and crept to the fireplace. She had become thoroughly chilled while making her way to Curzon's studio.

I wonder if he will come here today? She held her hands out to the flames. *Should I ask him to help me?* She had seen very little of Harrison Curzon during the last two weeks, and far too much of His Grace, the Duke of Winkham. To her intense surprise and alarm, the duke had liked her father, whose appearance in London had been an unwelcome complication, though Bella was delighted to be reunited with her mother.

He and the duke shared an interest in breeding pigs. The two of them had even made a brief visit to the Eardley home in Hertfordshire so that Winkham could view

Bertram Eardley's swine farm. He had been truly impressed by both her father's stock and the fine quarters he provided them.

He had also been rhapsodic about one of Bella's paintings.When she was twelve, she had painted the portrait of her father's prize boar as his birthday present.

Having warmed her hands sufficiently, Bella turned her backside to the fire, running her hands over the satin breeches to see how wet they were. She stopped, a small gasp escaping her lips, upon seeing the long, lean frame of Harrison Curzon sprawled upon the sofa.

His chest rose and fell regularly. He was sound asleep. *How beautiful he is*, Bella thought, moving forward silently to study the sleeping man. Even in repose, with his mouth slightly open, there was an aura of leashed power about him. After a few minutes of rapt contemplation of his masculine form, Bella had an idea. Softly, as silently as possible, she made her way to her portfolio and took out of it a large drawing pad and a box containing her chalks. Tiptoeing back with equal care, she leaned against the wall beside the fireplace and braced the drawing pad on her thigh. With swift, sure strokes she began a pastel portrait of Harrison Curzon.

The sound of chalk scratching across paper was the first thing Harrison was aware of as he came awake. He opened his eyes cautiously, smiling at the sight of Isabella Eardley in her page's uniform, her small tongue protruding from the side of her mouth, concentrating deeply on her paper. She looked up, her eyes trained on the lower part of his anatomy, and he suddenly became aware of the perfectly normal but in the circumstances highly embarrassing condition he was displaying. He sat up abruptly, startling her so much that she dropped her sketch pad.

"Oh!" She put her hand to her heart. "I thought you were asleep."

"And so I was." He rested his folded hands casually on his lap.

"Well, please don't get up. I wasn't finished."

"I think you were." He leaned forward and picked up her sketch, curious to see just how anatomically correct it was.

It was *very* anatomically correct. Curzon's eyebrows shot up. "My, my."

Bella flushed a bright pink. "I never meant for you to see it."

"And *I* never meant for *you* to see *it*. What can you be about, coming here alone? That is . . ." He half stood to glance behind him. "Just as I suspected. Completely unattended. Do you want to be ruined, Isabella?"

She met his eyes defiantly. "Perhaps I do. If I were ruined, Winky Winkham would go away and leave me alone. I am afraid my father is going to make me marry him, and I don't want to. I don't want to marry anyone, and particularly not that dull-witted slow-top who sees nothing in me but an ornament and a breeder."

"What makes you think your father would insist on Winkham? You have dozens of young men buzzing around you."

Bella sighed. "But his is the highest title. My father worships the idea of my being a duchess. He is discouraging all of my other suitors."

"So you have come here to get me to ruin you!" Curzon scowled furiously at her. "Have you given any thought at all to what that would do to me, Isabella? My father intends me to have a career as a politician and statesman. Not much chance of that if I take to ruining eligible young females."

She shook her head mournfully. "No, I see it won't serve. That wasn't what I had in mind, anyway. I only stopped here because I was so very cold. You see, I am running away."

Chapter Nine

Harrison shook his head at her, half amused. "That is ridiculous. I am sure if you appeal to that dragon of a grandmother of yours, she will not allow you to be forced into a marriage. And what about your mother? Hasn't she any influence on her husband?"

"My mother thinks Winky is a good choice for me because he is not apt to beat me. My grandmother thinks he loves me, and that I would be a fool to pass up a chance to marry a man who truly cares for me."

Curzon ran his hand over his face, scrubbing at his eyes with long fingers. "Perhaps her opinion, at least, has some merit."

"Her opinion is the most misguided of all!"

"You don't believe in love, then? I confess I have my doubts about the fabled emotion."

"It isn't that. But Winky *doesn't* love me. How could he when he doesn't know me? If he understood anything at all about me, he'd understand how important art is to me. But he doesn't. I think he hasn't enough matter in his brain-box to do so."

"He would forbid you to paint?"

Isabella's laugh was sardonic. "By no means. When I attempted to explain my artistic ambitions, he assured me that I could paint portraits of all his prize pigs. He thinks me a female Stubbs, and believe me, that is the highest praise he is capable of bestowing."

Harrison shook his head. "I can see why you lack enthusiasm for a future of porcine portraiture."

"You are the only one I have ever met who understands

me. No, that's not entirely true. My governesses did—Eden Henderson and Mary Fenton. I feel so alone!"

Harry drew her down beside him on the sofa and patted her hands comfortingly. "Isabella, I do understand, and I share your frustration and dismay. But running away is a desperate course."

"I am desperate."

"Where do you think to go? Have you any relatives or friends who would shelter you? What about money?"

"Who would hide me from my family? I shall have to hide myself. When I am twenty-five, I will come into a legacy from my grandfather. If I can remain unmarried until then, I will be able to live independently and devote myself to my art."

Harrison scanned her face. She had the dewy fresh complexion of a child. "And you are . . . what did you tell me . . . sixteen?"

She shook her head vehemently. "I am almost eighteen."

"Ah! A great age indeed. Only eight years to go until you are independent."

"I know what I will do until then. I will find work adding watercolors to aquatints. There must be a great demand for good watercolorists, considering how many artists are publishing engravings. Then there are fashion plates and tourists' guides. Why, Mr. Ackermann alone must employ dozens. . . ."

Harrison frowned. "My poor child. How very naive you are. He does indeed employ dozens, most of them children. It is a very meager living, I assure you."

"I don't care," Isabella declared passionately. "I don't require luxury. All I need is a room with good northern light, and—"

"To make enough to support yourself you would have to work from dawn to dusk in the printmakers' studios. The unfortunate people who earn their living that way usually live in crowded tenements, a half dozen or more to a single room. You would never see the light of day. You wouldn't earn enough to eat well, much less purchase art supplies."

"I . . . I don't believe you." She flew off the sofa and turned to face him defiantly. "You are as bad as the rest, telling me what I can't do instead of helping me find what I can do!"

"I am only facing reality. I suppose I could assist you financially—"

"No! I don't want your charity!"

"—but think of the scandal if the source of your income were discovered. And think of your family's heartbreak if you were to disappear for eight years."

"They aren't thinking of *my* heartbreak! I was wrong about you. You don't really understand, how could you? You can paint as much as you like. No one can tell you—"

"You are wrong there, my girl. My family has never understood or approved of my painting. My friends would ridicule me if they understood its importance to me. And very soon I shall have to give it up for a career in politics or an even more boring life managing my father's estates and investments. He has decided, you see, that I need useful employment."

Bella's eyes widened. "No! You mustn't. Surely a grown man cannot be forced—"

"You cannot be ignorant of the power of the purse." He lifted his eyebrows inquiringly.

"Oh, no, Harrison. Would they cut you off without a cent if you defied them?"

Harry lowered his head and stared at his hands. "Perhaps. I calculate that my income would be less than three hundred pounds a year if my father cut up stiff. I spend that much in an ordinary week. Of course, I could earn something from my paintings, and I can learn to live without luxuries. Money is less of a stumbling block to me than loyalty. He has ever been a loving father to me, generous to the point of indulgence. My mother is a dear creature, too. They are both eager to see me wed and established in some sort of career that is comprehensible to them. You may be able to turn your back on your family without pain, but I cannot."

Bella sat back down beside him and put her hands over his. "Harrison Curzon! Everyone thinks you are a care-for-nothing, but you are not, not at all."

"No, I am not." Harry lifted his head. Bella's blue eyes were shining with something more than mere sympathy. And even more than understanding, though she clearly did understand. Not for the first time he wondered if the little chit was in love with him. He reached out and cupped her head in his hand. *She is too young. Still . . . Winkham is almost forty, and they want her to marry him.*

"Let me think about your plight, Isabella. Perhaps I can find a way to help you. Do you think your family would let me call on you?"

Bella blinked rapidly. Somehow her thinking processes had stopped when his large hand had engulfed the side of her head. "I . . . perhaps. Papa would welcome the opportunity to meet you, I expect, for your family is the peak of the *ton*. But grandmother might object. She thinks you are the devil incarnate. I don't understand why."

Harry smiled wryly. "Let us just say I have developed something of a reputation. Your grandmother is one of the custodians of the moral order."

Bella's full mouth tilted upward. "I heard you once had three high flyers in your keeping at one time. Is that true?"

"Who on earth would tell you such a thing?"

"Winky. He admires you greatly, you know."

"That gossiping fool. You shouldn't even know of such things, child."

"I am not a child. I am small, but I am a woman grown, I'll have you to know!"

His eyes raked her. She had not troubled this time to pad out the page's jacket to make herself look chubby. Dampness caused it to drape her curves from chest to below her waist, where the satin breeches snugly delineated her hips. The wet ruffles on her shirt were plastered to a very agreeably rounded bosom.

"Indeed you are. And perhaps just now too much temptation for a rake like me. Go home, Bella. Let me think on your situation and see if I can find a way to help you."

Bella felt a flush run through her at this frankly admiring appraisal. She was embarrassed but exhilarated to have him take note of her as a woman at last. She batted her eyelashes provocatively. "*Could* I tempt you?"

Take care, Harrison, he warned himself. *Your amatory instincts are far too easily aroused. This child has no idea the fire she is playing with.*

He picked up her discarded sketch pad and looked over her drawing of him before raising his eyes to her. In an insinuating tone he drawled, "Yes, you could, little hoyden. And the results could be disastrous for you. You had best leave before I kiss you soundly."

She drew back in mock alarm. "A fate worse than death." She hoped he couldn't hear her heart thudding against her chest.

"More than one gently bred female has thought so!"

Bella began to be a little nervous of the gleam in his eyes. Though she had dreamed of him making love to her, air-dreaming and having him here, so potently male, sitting inches from her, were two different things. She hastened to change the subject. "Before I go, will you let me finish my sketch?"

"Certainly not." He tore the drawing from her book and

crossed to the fire. "Even a rake like me draws the line at indecent paintings of himself."

"Don't!" Bella launched herself at him, but he held her off easily as he fed her drawing into the flames.

"Blast you. Blast and damn! I never have a chance to draw men. How am I to know how to represent the male anatomy? I am not allowed to attend life drawings, and I would totally scandalize my grandmother if I hired a model. I needed that study!"

Curzon held off the blows she was attempting to rain on him. "I'm sorry, Bella, but that drawing was beyond the line, and you know it."

She gave up her exertions and walked to the window, to stare out at the clouds obscuring the sky so effectively the sun might as well never have risen. She was fighting tears, and once again Curzon felt that wave of emotion that he had often experienced in her presence. But this time he didn't know how to assist her. He could not even try to comfort her, for fear of where it might lead.

Choking back her tears, Bella turned to him. "You must pose for me again before I go. It won't be indecent. I just need an opportunity to work on drawing the male figure."

"I think you should leave now, Bella."

"After you pose for me."

"It isn't a good idea."

She cocked her head pertly. "I know. I'll give you that kiss you wanted if you'll pose for me nude." At the shock on his face she hastened to add, "Not completely nude. You can drape your . . . you know."

A rising tension in his . . . "you know" . . . made Harrison determined to oust her. How could he get rid of this determined creature? *I have frightened off two other gently bred females with passionate kisses. Bella will surely run from me as well.*

"Very well, child. Come here."

Surprised, but determined to succeed, she bounded to his side. "You mean it? A kiss for a pose. Is it a bargain?"

He held out his hand. "Let us shake on it."

She put her small hand in his, excited and alarmed all at once. Not only would she have her drawing, she would have a kiss. Would it be anything as wonderful as in her dreams? In spite of her nervous awareness of his overpowering physical presence, she felt a flush of desire surging through her body.

She lifted her head and pursed her lips much as Virginia had done at the Chelsea Physic Gardens. Harrison felt his heart give a lurch such as he had not felt on that occasion. *She is brave, adorable, and naive as a kitten. One kiss will awaken her to the danger she courts by being alone with a man.* Thus justifying his behavior to himself, he pulled her abruptly into his arms. He lifted her off her feet and kissed her hard, fully intending to alarm her.

To his surprise, she didn't resist him at all. Her arms quickly came round his neck. She clung tightly to him. At the feel of her curvaceous form molded against him, he groaned and drew his head away.

"Bella! For God's sake."

Large blue eyes examined him in amazement. "So that is what a kiss from a man is like. It isn't anything at all like a kiss from my parents or grandmother."

"No, it isn't. Now you know why you must leave immediately." *Put her down. Now!* He urged himself. But he didn't put her down.

Nor did she seek to escape. Instead, she wrapped her arms around him more tightly. "It was of all things wonderful. Kiss me again."

Let her go, you fool, before you do something you will despise yourself for. Harrison unwrapped her arms and let her slide to the floor. "I don't think that would be wise."

Bella tilted her head back, still pressing her body against

him. It felt so wonderful to be this near him. She had not realized the feel, the scent of a man could be so intoxicating. "Have I earned my modeling privilege yet?"

"Not quite," he snarled, bending his head to take her lips again. This time he would give her a disgust of him for sure.

But when he thrust his tongue past her lips, instead of resisting him, she opened her mouth. Her guttural moan inflamed his passions, and before he knew what he was doing, he had carried her to the sofa and borne her down upon it, kissing her passionately again and again.

Bella matched his passion. She quickly learned to meet his tongue with her own, and thrust her hips up against him in a sure sign of feminine responsiveness. When he lifted his head, intending to pull away, she wove her hands into his curling blond hair and tugged him nearer.

"I am lost. So are you, Miss Isabella Eardley," he whispered harshly against her neck as he slipped his hand inside her jacket. Soft, encouraging sounds were her only answer as he caressed her curves.

The sensations he was making her feel enthralled Bella. She was on fire, and she wanted, needed this magnificent man to put out the flames.

As he tugged on her breeches, he whispered in her ear, "At least this will solve your problem, little one."

"Hmmmm?"

"We'll be married. You won't have to worry about *me* preventing you from painting."

Bella stiffened beneath him. He moaned. She was going to stop him. He wasn't sure he could stop. "No, sweetheart, don't be frightened. I will be gentle—"

"Harry, no. This is not what I want. Well, I do want it, but we mustn't. Oh, please! Stop before it is too late."

Her frantic tone reached him. He shoved away from her and fell from the couch, welcoming the distraction of bruising contact with the floor.

Her curls even more tumbled than usual, and her lips swollen from his kisses, Bella leaned over and held out her arms. "Did you hurt yourself? I didn't mean to push you off the sofa."

He shrank away from her. "If you don't want us to make love, get up from there and get out of here this instant."

She drew back at his furious tone. "Please forgive me. I do want to make love with you. But it would only lead to one of two things. Either I would become your mistress, in which case people would pay more attention to the scandal than to my paintings, or I would become your wife, in which case I'd spend my life breeding and giving dinner parties for boring old politicians. I . . . I don't want to be a wife, Harrison. Not even your wife." For the first time in his presence she burst into actual sobs.

He watched her cry for a minute, fighting the impulse to take her in his arms and comfort her. That would lead to the very situation she was trying to avoid! He rose reluctantly to his feet. "So you reject me, too. Might as well. It's the fashionable thing to do."

She lifted her head from her hands. "No, Harry, it isn't like that. I . . . I think I love you."

"Love me! Ha! You're too self-centered to love anyone. As am I. We both care more for our art than any person."

"That's not fair to either of us. You care about your father. And I *do* care about you. But don't you see, I'll never succeed as an artist if I accept the usual role of a female. There's no way for a woman to do both. I've always known that. Oh, please don't glare at me so. It isn't as if you are in love with me. You just said yourself that you didn't even believe in love." She leaned forward and stroked a soft, gentle finger over his frown lines.

Bella's touch burned Harrison like fire. He retreated as if she had the plague. "Since you won't leave, I must. I've ever forced myself on an unwilling woman before, but I can't answer for myself if I stay here."

He stomped to the door and threw on his greatcoat. Without a backward glance he slammed the door back on its hinges and banged his way down the stairway.

Bella sat for a long time in his studio, shivering with frustration and sorrow in spite of the warmth of the fire. Finally, she stood, straightened her disheveled clothes, gathered up her sketch pad, put it in her portfolio, and left the room, closing the door softly, regretfully, behind her.

Chapter Ten

After a slow start because of the period of mourning that had been observed for King George III, by early June the season was well and truly underway. "The ball is a success, don't you think?" Millicent Curzon looked anxiously up at her older son.

"Of course, Mama. Your ball always is. An invitation to The Elms can always lure the *ton* away from London's many lesser entertainments."

His mother was pleased with his assessment, which was based on the fact that the room was too hot and so crowded that dancers on the floor kept crashing into on-lookers ranged around it. There was a din of voices so loud the music could barely be heard.

Harrison Curzon wished he could be anywhere but here. His father had insisted he attend, however, to meet the Cranbournes' daughter Alice. "Not only are they old and very dear friends, son, but their daughter is highly eligible and since you have yet to find a bride for yourself . . ."

So here he was, beginning a country dance with Alice Cranbourne, though they could hear so little of the music it was difficult to coordinate their steps with the other dancers, and the figures of the dance often sent them mingling with the milling throng at the edge of the ballroom.

Miss Cranbourne turned gracefully beneath his arm. *At least she is tall*, he told himself. *Much preferable to dancing with a midget.* But he was giving himself Spanish coin, for his eyes kept straying to Isabella Eardley, dancing in the next set.

She looked unusually pretty tonight in a daffodil yellow satin slip draped with a white lace overdress. Some of her golden curls had been mounded on the crown of her head and encircled by an arrangement of silk flowers. The ringlets left around her face bounced as she moved.

She was dancing with the Duke of Winkham. *Winky is a clumsy fellow*, Curzon thought, and then tromped on the foot of his partner. "Excuse me, Miss Cranbourne. There is so much noise and confusion in here . . ."

"And so many pretty misses to look at," she sniffed, turning her high-bridged nose up at him.

Curzon knew he had slighted her. He also knew if he exerted himself he could still turn her up sweet. But he wasn't interested in making the effort. He only grinned at her and shrugged his shoulders. They finished the dance in silence, and he retreated to the sidelines, determined to stay there unless he could manage a dance with Bella.

He never would have expected to secure a dance with her, given her relatives' patent disapproval of him, except for a peculiar circumstance: the Duke of Winkham continued to admire him. He attempted to ape him in matters of dress; he had purchased a team as like Curzon's as he could, and hitched them to a curricle of the same style and color. He had even taken to copying Curzon's unique manner of tying his cravat, with enough success that others had noticed and begun teasing him about it.

It was not unusual for young cubs attempting to acquire some town bronze to imitate him. He found it unusually irritating this time, perhaps because Winkham, far from being a young cub, was older than himself. But he had a rather devious reason for tolerating Winkham. The acquaintance allowed him to speak occasionally with Isabella, whom the duke escorted frequently. This evening he hoped it would give him an opportunity to dance with her, granted by Winkham while the duchess was otherwise engaged.

With the difference in our height, we'll look a deuced odd couple, he thought. But he felt an urgent need to know how the little hoyden was doing, and what kind of accommodation she had made with her family. The few chances he had had to speak to her had always been in company, where they could not discuss her problems.

When the promenade ended, Curzon at last saw his opening. *Fate is with me. All of her dragons are on the other side of the room*, he thought as he quickly made his way to Isabella and Winkham.

He clapped Winkham on the shoulder. "Well met, old chap."

The duke's eyes shone at this notice from the man who had become for him the epitome of the town beau. "Harrison! Grand party, old man."

"Not a bad do." Harrison winked at Bella. "Have you tried the lobster paté? That new chef of Mama's has outdone himself."

The duke was an avid epicurean. "Shall we make our way to the buffet, Bella?"

"I was hoping you might dance with me, Miss Eardley?"

Bella lowered her eyes. "I can't eat lobster, Winky. It makes me break out in spots even to think of it."

"Then by all means dance with Harry. I'll be back shortly." The duke turned with a single-minded zeal in the direction of the magnificent buffet Harrison's mother had laid out in the salon adjoining the ballroom.

"Harrison! At last!" Bella seized Curzon's arm eagerly when he offered it to her. "I thought I would never be able to talk privately with you again, not that we are private, but . . ."

He nodded. "A waltz in a crowded room is about as close to privacy as we will be able to manage."

Suddenly serious and a little sad, she said, "I thought you might at least call on me, to see if I returned home safely that day."

"I did call on you. I was told that you were ill. My reception was so frosty I dared not repeat the attempt. Your father was as cold as your grandmother. I expect she warned him against me."

"It is very wicked of them. They never told me."

"I called that very afternoon, overwhelmed with guilt and fear that you had gone on to carry out your plans to run away."

She lifted her small round chin proudly. "And so I did. I spoke to Mr. Ackermann, and even demonstrated my ability to watercolor to Mr. Archibald, who is producing a tour guide to the Cotswolds. He was willing to hire me, but the pittance he offered me was so small, I had to admit to myself that you were right. There was no way to keep myself decently by my own labors. Besides that, he saw through my disguise instantly. At least I think he did, for he pinched my bottom and leered at me, though he kept on calling me 'young Master Clarence.'"

Harrison shuddered. A young person as lovely as Bella was in danger, whether male or female. "It appears that you have decided Winky is the better alternative."

"I have not! They think it, but I will not marry! My father doesn't know me at all."

He looked down admiringly at the tiny, determined creature. "I almost believe you will evade parson's mousetrap.

"Will you do the same?"

"I never said I wanted to. I am, in fact, actively seeking a partner, as I promised my father I would do."

"Oh." Bella frowned and looked away. It seemed to him that this intelligence had upset her, which caused his own spirits to rise.

Virginia whirled by on Gilbert's arms. Their happiness was apparent. "I expect an announcement from the battling cousins any day. Have you had a chance to speak with her?"

"Briefly. Her mother blames everything on me, you know. And I expect I did start it all, but she would be dismayed to know how able a conspirator her daughter is."

They both laughed, and their eyes met in mutual understanding. A thrill shot through Isabella. "Oh, Harry, I miss you. How I wish I could come and paint with you."

His full lips twitched. "And here I was hoping you wished to come and do something much more interesting with me."

"Wicked man," she said without the slightest hint of censure. "But you are right. We *do* have unfinished business!"

"So we do." Curzon felt his blood heating at the thought of their interrupted lovemaking.

"You left me without posing for me. I mean to collect my winnings someday!"

"I shall look forward to that day, Miss Eardley." Curzon's lopsided smile suggested that he was looking forward to much more. Bella's eyes widened; she met his gaze without flinching. The long look they shared seemed to singe the air between them. They were jostled by several other couples leaving the floor before they realized the dance had ended.

"We are attracting attention," he said reluctantly, taking her hand and placing it on his arm to lead her back to Winky. The duke had an anxious look on his face.

Just then a raucous burst of laughter turned their attention to the door of the card room, where Isabella's father was entering in the company of several of the *ton*'s high rollers.

"It appears your father has begun to make a place for himself in society," Curzon observed.

"That does not speak very well for the *ton*, does it?", she responded in a cynical tone. "Hullo, Winky. It is so terribly hot in here. May we walk on the terrace?"

Whatever scolding words the duke had been about to

utter concerning their behavior on the dance floor went unsaid as he grasped the treat being offered him. Flashing a triumphant grin at Curzon, he led Isabella away.

I wonder if she'll kiss him as passionately as she did me, Curzon thought, surprised at the fury that surged through him at the idea. But as it had so often this wet, cool spring, it was raining fiercely outside, which was one reason the ballroom had been shut up so tightly in spite of the heat generated by so many bodies. The pair were only on the terrace long enough to turn around and come back in, the duke looking solicitously at a shivering Isabella. It was Harry's turn to grin. Not for a minute did he believe the rain had slipped Bella's mind.

It was customary for a gentleman to call upon his dance partners the day after a ball. Curzon waited until another of Bella's partners started up the steps to Carminster House. Joining him, he succeeded in gaining entrance to the duchess's drawing room. He would have been better pleased with himself for outwitting the duchess had his presence seemed to please Bella.

She was sitting with her mother and grandmother, entertaining half a dozen of the *ton*'s young bucks. At the sight of Harrison Curzon joining them, Mr. Eardley looked furious. The duchess was as frosty as ever. He would not have shrunk from the dislike of these dragons if Isabella had been encouraging. But she looked at him as he imagined a rabbit might at a hound.

Her oddly chastened, subdued manner disturbed him greatly. *It would seem that she was punished for our indiscreet behavior on the dance floor last night*. The fury that engulfed him at the thought of Bella being mistreated revealed to him the inescapable truth of what had been happening to him in the last few weeks. There was much more than mere lust or interest in art between himself and this tiny, dynamic young woman: he was falling in love with Miss Isabella Eardley.

As he left the duchess's drawing room, Harrison promised himself that he would find a way to rescue her from the clutches of these cold-blooded relatives and marry her, whether she wished it or not.

"I take it that your introduction to Miss Cranbourne last night did not result in love at first sight."

"Nor second or third, Father. A mutual antipathy sprang up between us that I felt no urge to dispel."

"You have dismissed one by one each of the eligible females your mother and I have presented to you thus far. I begin to despair of you, Harry. It is as I feared: you have spent too many hours in the arms of the muslin company. Gently bred females seem too tame and dull for you."

Harry lounged back in his chair, pleased to be able to meet at least one of his father's requirements. "Actually, I have some good news for you, Pater. I have found a young lady who is not at all tame. In fact, I am in love."

Sir Randall's surprise was evident. "That is good news, indeed. But who can she be? Since I have not seen you so much as dance two dances with the same young female, I cannot imagine . . ."

"I haven't danced twice with her because her family doesn't approve of me."

"I knew that might happen. Your reputation . . ."

"My reputation is only partially responsible. Another problem is my lack of prospects for a title."

"Ah! Then perhaps you will be pleased to know that the crown has in mind for me an obscure earldom that is in abeyance and likely to become extinct any minute. We are very distantly related to Miss Griselda Moran, who might have revived the earldom of Bramtham had she married and borne a son, but at eighty she seems unlikely to do so. She hovers now at death's door . . ."

Harrison jumped up, a smile lighting his features. "That is famous. Heir to an earl! Just what is needed. Not as high as a dukedom, but surely enough for that mushroom of a father of hers."

"Mushroom? Harry, you led me to believe the girl is suitable."

"Oh, she is. Granddaughter of the Duke of Carminster. You can't get much higher in the *ton* than that. The remaining problem is that she fancies herself unwilling to marry. However, I think a slightly indiscreet walk in someone's darkened gardens might change her mind."

Sir Randall began shaking his head vehemently. "Not that Eardley chit! No, no, Harry. She won't do. She won't do at all."

Harrison scowled. "You hardly know her. I grant you she is an original, but—"

"It's nothing to do with the child. She is pretty and I know nothing against her behavior. But that father of hers." He suppressed a shudder. "Just the thought of being related to Bertram Eardley makes me nauseated. A more pushing, annoying fellow I have never met. When I tell you what he and that fool the Duke of Winkham are getting up to, you will realize the ineligibility of the connection."

"Would you perhaps be referring to Winky's proposal in the House of Lords that the government pay subsidies to encourage the building of raised brick pigsties? The Porcine Palace Bill, the papers are calling it."

Sir Randall nodded curtly. "That's it. When the poor of our country are starving, and our brave war veterans sleeping under hedgerows, they want all Englishmen to be taxed so rich men can build mansions for pigs!"

Harry tried to suppress his smile, with limited success. "I suppose you pointed out to Mr. Eardley the folly of such a bill?"

"I made sure he knew that I think he and his like are the swine, feeding from the government trough!"

Curzon stroked his lips thoughtfully. *That explains Eardley's poorly disguised hostility this afternoon.* "Then snub him. I don't care, and I seriously doubt Bella will either. She speaks of him rather disparagingly."

"One cannot ignore such a near connection. Gad. Think what having such a father-in-law would do to your political career. Tell me, how have you managed to fall in love with her? I didn't even know that you were acquainted."

Harrison smiled reminiscently. "She descended on me like a whirlwind one day, wanting to take art lessons." He proceeded to tell his father of his relationship with Isabella.

"Worse and worse. A hoyden. Why, she may not even be chaste. A chit who will slip her lead that way may have gotten into God knows how many compromising situations."

Harry shook his head. "I have good reason to know she has not succumbed to that particular temptation, sir."

His father looked at him, thunderstruck. "Never say you've already thrown your leg over her?"

"Absolutely not! But it was a close run thing. If anyone were able to get past her determination to devote herself to art instead of the usual female role, I flatter myself it would be me. She is chaste."

"Chaste, but not virtuous."

Harrison's hands fisted on the arm of his chair. "Have a care. You are speaking of the woman I love."

"I should have known you'd select a female who is as like your doxies as possible."

"She is like them only in that she promises to give me as

much pleasure in bed as any female ever born. But because she is passionate, that does not mean she is promiscuous."

Sir Randall left his chair to stand moodily before the window that overlooked the lake. The Greek temple seemed to glow where it was struck by the setting sun, but the sight gave him no pleasure. At last he turned, to find his son leaning against the mantelpiece, his arms folded, waiting for his response.

"I am sorry, Harry, but I cannot accept such as she into our family. You will just have to—"

Harry straightened, his face grim. "That is a deal too bad, sir, for I love Isabella Eardley. She is the first female I have ever been able to say that about, and I daresay the last. I will marry her or no one!"

"Then I shall just have to rely on Patrick to carry on my new title, shan't I?"

Father and son stared antagonistically at one another. Finally, Harry broke the silence. "That might be very much to the good, sir. I find the role of dutiful, obedient son begins to sit ill upon my shoulders. You seem to forget I am not a child for you to command."

"Because you insist on behaving as one."

"This is getting us nowhere. I have an engagement. I must get back to London. I bid you good day, sir."

"You will stop in to say hello to your mother and grandmother first."

"I think not, sir. Not today. Mother knows me too well. T'would only distress her." So saying, Harrison left his father's presence, his heart heavy.

Chapter Eleven

"Mama, society seems to agree with you." Bella studied her mother's formerly gaunt, strained features with interest. Since her mother and father had come to reside with the duchess, Seraphina Eardley's face had filled out, as had the rest of her. She looked ten years younger.

"I have been enjoying myself wonderfully," Bella's mother agreed.

"Papa and Grandmama have gotten along so well during this visit. I am glad they have learned to deal well together, for your sake."

To her surprise, her mother bit her lip and looked away, seeming to fight tears. "What is it, Mama?"

"N-nothing, Bella. Only . . ." Her mother seemed to be looking everywhere but directly at her. "I wonder . . . do you . . . that is . . . will you . . ."

"Mama!"

"If His Grace offers for you, will you have him?" Mrs. Eardley met her daughter's eyes at last, her own pleading.

Bella frowned. *Why, she acts as if her very life depends upon my accepting him.* "Mama, you know I don't wish to marry."

"But Bella, you must."

Bella shook her head. "I won't."

Mrs. Eardley slumped back against the sofa where she sat in the cozy, small parlor. "Your father . . ."

"He may bluff and bluster and threaten, but he daren't force me. Grandmama would never countenance it. She would see that he was cut entirely by society if—Mama!"

Bella watched in consternation as her mother sprang up and fled the room.

"Well, that is of all things peculiar," she announced to the furniture as she, too, stood up, intending to follow her mother.

"There you are, Bella!" Her father entered the room in his usual blustery way. "The duke is waiting for you. Had you forgotten you are to call on his great-aunt with him today?"

"No, Papa, I haven't forgotten. Mother and I were deep in conversation."

"What about?" Her father looked at her suspiciously, uneasily.

"I was complimenting her on looking so well, now you and Grandmama have come to an accommodation."

Mr. Eardley's eyes narrowed. "What do you know about that?"

Bella didn't reply. *Something is afoot*, she thought with a sinking feeling.

"Has that feather-brained wife of mine told you . . . ?"

"She told me nothing, Father. I have simply observed that you and Grandmama do not quarrel as much as you were wont to do, and Mama seems much more relaxed as a result."

"Ah." Her father rocked back on his heels and smiled slyly at her. "Perfectly true. The old besom has mellowed toward me, and not before time, neither. Come along, missy. You can't keep a duke cooling his heels, you know!"

Bella knew better than to try to learn anything more from her father, but as she drew on her gloves, she vowed to question her grandmother at the first opportunity.

The Duke of Winkham turned impatiently as Bella entered the drawing room. "My cattle have been standing for a quarter of an hour. Let us be off at once."

"Good morning to you, too." Bella lifted her chin and turned on her heel, walking across the foyer so quickly the duke had to run to catch up to her. He attempted to take her elbow, but she jerked it free. *You don't own me yet*, she thought defiantly.

Bella allowed the duke to hand her up. When he had taken his seat, his tiger sprang away as if the team would run over him. But they placidly awaited their driver's signal before moving calmly into the street.

"D'you like m'new team?" the duke asked her eagerly.

Bella scanned the sorrel horses indifferently. He hadn't even noticed she was in a pet, much less attempted to soothe her.

The duke's obtuseness was one of her complaints against him. He was so totally wrapped up in himself, and so completely confident of his success with her, that he often behaved as if she had no independent existence at all. *And we aren't even engaged yet, much less married.*

"Fine as fivepence, ain't they?" Winkham enthused, not even taking note of her silence. "Got 'em at Tat's last week. Remarkably like Curzon's pair, ain't they?"

"Right down to the placid, job-horse disposition," she replied nastily.

"Job horses! Silly goose! Harrison Curzon is a nonesuch. Famous for his cattle. Wonder if my pair would take his?"

"I admit I know little of these things, but I had not thought Mr. Curzon's pair was racing stock." Bella noted with irritation that her heart had begun racing like a frightened thoroughbred at the mere mention of Harrison's name.

"I cannot believe Curzon would have a pair that wasn't fast. They're just well-trained, as are these. First-rate horsemen like Curzon and me don't look for surface show, or mistake restive, ill-disciplined cattle for prime bloods."

"I see." Bella shrugged indifferently and let her mind wander.

"There he is. We'll see 'em together now."

She jerked back to attention, to realize that they were

well into Hyde Park, with its usual frenzy of traffic at the fashionable hour. Ahead of them was Harrison Curzon, driving alone. The duke flicked up his team and drove alongside.

"Ho, Harrison. What do you think of my new team? They were Arnold Lanscombe's. He had them auctioned at Tattersall's. Ringers for yours, eh?"

Curzon's full lips lifted in a slight sneer as he turned at the sound of the duke's voice. His expression changed to one of pleasure when he saw Bella. He tipped his hat to her and then pretended to study the team beside him judiciously. "I had not realized Arnold had cattle worth buying."

Winkham grinned. "As you see! They are astonishingly like yours, are they not? Bella was wondering if they were as fast as your pair."

Surprised, Curzon shifted his gaze to Isabella, who replied in a tone as bored as she could make it, "Why yes, I am quite on pins and needles to know."

"I can see that you are. Hmmm. Perhaps we shall try them out sometime soon, eh, Winky?"

"One of your famous races. I should say so! When and where?"

Harrison studied Bella thoughtfully before turning to the duke. He wished she were up beside him instead of driving with this fawning bore. Since her family clearly would not let him court her openly, he had to think of some way to see her.

"More important, what will be the stakes? Join me at White's tonight for dinner. We'll think of something to make it worthwhile."

"I say! Excellent!" Winkham looked as if he might explode at this invitation by the man he admired, envied, and sought to emulate. "You see, Bella. Did I not say Curzon was fond of racing?"

Bella cocked her head, studying Harrison's sparkling eyes speculatively. "I'm not entirely sure I do see, Winky. But I shall look forward to hearing the outcome."

"Grandmama, I need to talk to you."

The duchess looked up from her fashion magazine and smiled welcomingly. "Sit beside me, child."

Bella settled on the sofa and politely admired the fashion plate her grandmother pointed out to her before launching into her inquisition. "Grandmama, Mother was behaving most peculiarly this morning. I commented on how well she is looking, and on how well you and Papa are dealing with one another, and I thought she was going to burst into tears. She asked me if I would accept Winky's proposal, and ran out of the room when I said no. Papa jumped as if I had pinched him when I told him what had happened."

The duchess surprised Bella by looking away. Those piercing blue eyes rarely flinched. "Your mother *is* looking well, and happy, isn't she?" she asked softly.

"Yes, but . . ."

"Aren't you glad to see her thus?"

"You know I am, but . . ."

"It is in your power to make her so for the rest of her life."

Bella felt the hairs stand on the back of her neck as if menaced by some unseen danger. "What do you mean?"

The duchess looked at her hands, then entwined her fingers before lifting her eyes to meet Bella's. "Your father has agreed to allow her to remain here with me. He will give her a legal separation, if only—"

"You have bargained for her life, with mine!" Hot tears stung her eyes as the truth hit Bella.

"I have only agreed to see you well married, which I would have done in any case."

"Even though I made it clear to you that I wished to remain single!"

"That is an impossibility. Now, Bella, I am going to be frank with you. It is not just that marriage is a woman's proper sphere. You are a very feminine creature. You will want a man eventually. Perhaps now you are too young and innocent to realize that a woman can be tempted by needs that only a man can meet, but one day you will discover it. Your family must see you safely married, or you will find yourself enamored of some unsuitable person, perhaps led into a scandalous life."

Bella blushed at the memory of Curzon's kisses, his hands on her all-too-eager body. She certainly hadn't been immune to his masculine appeal. *But I did say no*, she told herself fiercely, conveniently forgetting that her reluctance had been brought out by Harry's suggestion that they marry, not by his seduction.

"I know something of the temptation you speak of, Grandmama, and I know I can resist it. I want to concentrate on studying and painting. How could I, and be at the beck and call of some man, or always be breeding?"

The duchess took her hand and tried to soothe her by stroking it. "You fail to realize that you are a considerable heiress. Even if you were that rare woman who is immune to masculine appeal, which I beg leave to doubt, you would be in constant danger of abduction by some adventurer intent on compromising you or carrying you to Gretna in order to secure your fortune. Marry the duke, my dear. He is not a bad man. Unlike your father, he has a gentle disposition, and can be managed."

Bella pulled her hand away. "No, Grandmama, he can't be managed. It is true he is unlikely to beat me. More likely, he will smother me in luxury and leisure. But he doesn't care enough for me to be managed by me. He is so selfish and self-involved that I really don't have any existence for him as a person. My main appeal for him is that I am well-connected, pretty, and shorter than he."

"I cannot see Winkham forbidding you to paint."

"No, but I can see him insisting that I not waste my time on landscapes or historical paintings when he has a stable and a barnyard full of prize animals to be portrayed."

The duchess laughed. "Ah, yes, his prize pigs."

Isabella jumped to her feet. "It is not so funny to me, Grandmama. You are asking me to live with that stupid man the rest of my life."

"I am asking you to save your mother from living the rest of her life with Bertram Eardley." The duchess's face expressed the ferocity of a mother protecting her child.

But who will protect me? Bella turned away from her grandmother despairingly. *I will have to run away again, and stay away this time.* Immediately on this defiant thought, though, came the recollection of her mother's dilemma. *But how can I face myself, knowing I have condemned my own mother to unhappiness?*

The duchess stood and smoothed down her dress briskly. "Now stop your maundering. It is not as if we were giving you to some horrible rake or ancient baron as your father meant to do. This way you have a home, a title, and a decent if unexciting husband. Incredible as it seems, he genuinely likes your father, which added to his lofty title, makes him a uniquely appealing match. Bertram will have his place assured in the *ton*, and I shall have Seraphina safely away from that monster her father married her to."

Bella looked up at her grandmother and sighed. "Very well, Grandmama. I will accept him, for mother's sake. But I won't marry him right away." Although she seemed to submit to her grandmother's wishes, Bella's mind was racing. *There must be a way to save mother without ruining my own life. I need time.* "I insist upon being allowed to finish my season before I accept him, and a respectable engagement period besides."

"Precious child. I knew you would agree." The duchess, rarely demonstrative, drew Bella into an enthusiastic embrace. "Let us go up and tell Seraphina at once."

The clank of cutlery, the chime of fine crystal, the low murmur of masculine voices filled in the awkward pause in the conversation after the Duke of Winkham heard the terms of Harrison Curzon's wager.

Red-faced with indignation, he started to struggle to his feet. "Far from agreeing to such a thing, I should call you out! The very idea of wagering my intended's virtue . . ."

Curzon leaned forward and jerked Winkham unceremoniously back into his chair. "Stupid chub. That is not what I said. I only asked you to provide the opportunity for me to spend a little time with her."

"You said 'take her into the dark paths of Vauxhall.' I am no Johnny Raw, not to know what goes on there."

"You have my word of honor that I will do her no harm. At the most I might steal a kiss is she is willing."

The duke relaxed a little. He had stolen a kiss from Bella once. She had protested vigorously, just as a decent girl ought. She would give Curzon short shrift. "Just that once, for a few minutes."

"Just that once. I want half an hour with her."

"Why do you not call on her and—"

"Her relatives guard her from me. My reputation is a bit ripe for them, I suppose. My intentions are honorable, though. I have hopes of marrying her. Since you aspire to the same hand, I will understand if you do not wish to wager—"

Winkham interrupted him hastily, not wanting to miss this chance to establish his reputation as a sporting buck. "The bet is on. Time with Bella against your team." He held out his hand. Curzon gripped it strongly, a slanted, mocking smile on his face.

Stung by the hint of contempt he read there, Winkham imitated Curzon's expression as nearly as he could. "Won't do you any good, you know. The fair Isabella is mine. We get along famously. You should have heard her raptures about my swine housing proposal. She said she was sure it was the most stunning maiden speech ever heard in the House of Lords! Besides, her father is title-mad, Curzon, and you haven't any."

"Then you've outfoxed me, haven't you, Winkham! I see you are an opponent to be reckoned with. One more thing." Curzon tossed down his napkin and stood. "No word of our agreement in the betting books. I do not want Isabella becoming the object of lewd speculation. If you must boast of it, put our wager down at a thousand guineas."

Winkham rubbed his hands together. "Excellent. Enough to make the *ton* take notice! Will you join me for some cards?"

"I had best get a good night's sleep, for I wouldn't want to lose my reputation as a whip."

"Noon tomorrow at the Hogmore Lane turnpike gate."

Curzon nodded, smiling lazily. "Until then."

Harrison was not surprised to find a small crowd gathered at the turnpike gate. Winkham was seeking to make a name for himself, which he could hardly do if he vanquished his opponent in secret. He was delighted to see Isabella and Virginia there, in Threlbourne's carriage, pastel parasols unfurled to protect them from the bright spring sunshine.

"What a fortunate fellow, to be surrounded with so much beauty," he greeted Gilbert, standing up in his carriage to bow to Virginia and Bella.

"Could have blown me over with a feather when I heard

you were to race that sorrel team of yours, Harry," Threl-bourne declared. "Though when I heard whose cattle Winky had purchased, that evened the odds."

"So you've put your money on the duke?"

"Huh! Any cattle you drive will be sound, even if not speedy. Lanscombe always had too much interest in his wardrobe to keep first-class animals. No, the smart money is on you!"

"I won't disappoint you!" Curzon winked wickedly at the two young women. Virginia's excitement flashed in her eyes. Bella was more composed. He looked closer at her. No, she looked positively blue-deviled.

"I do wish you could join them, Gil!" Virginia pouted prettily.

"Wouldn't be a fair race at all. Those grays of his are un-beatable." So saying, Curzon clicked to his horses and guided them to the starting point. They were to race to Hammersmith, turn their horses, and race back. The first one presenting himself at the Dun Cow Inn would be the winner.

At first it looked as if the duke would trounce Harrison. He plied his whip almost from the start, putting his team ahead early in the race. He arrived in Hammersmith well before his challenger. He yelped with glee as he met Curzon in the road back to London. "Might as well stop for tea, old man," he shouted.

But shortly thereafter his leader faltered, and then both horses slowed, nor would they continue to gallop no matter how hard the duke plied the whip. Curzon passed him eas-ily, coming into the Dun Cow's courtyard standing up, not even pushing his horses.

Thus it was that when Harrison Curzon joined the duke's party at Vauxhall two days later, Winkham stiffly bade him welcome, and made no demur when his rival asked Bella to stroll the gardens with him.

Puzzled by Winkham's acquiescence, she nevertheless accepted the invitation eagerly. Curzon led her slowly but inexorably to one of the dark walks, drawing her out as they progressed. "You look downpin, Bella. Is something wrong?"

"Other than Winkham and his friends being dead bores, you mean?"

"You looked almost this bleak that morning at the beginning of the race."

"That was before I knew you would win." She smiled up at him, but he had the feeling that her answer was less than candid.

He drew her into a small alcove that boasted a bench. There was no light except for that shed on them by a quarter moon. Suddenly realizing where their steps had carried them, Bella lifted her eyebrows.

"What are you about, Harry?"

He gave her a slow, lazy, decidedly wicked smile that made her toes tingle. "I haven't been able to keep my mind on my painting since that kiss we shared in my studio. Have you thought of it, midget?"

"I am not a midget," Bella fussed, but she sat by him as he wished her to do.

"Have you thought of my kisses, little amazon?"

"That's better!"

"Bella!" His voice was a low, urgent growl.

"I have, much good it will do either of us."

He slide his arm around her shoulders, urging her close to him. "Nonsense, for it tells us that we must repeat the experience."

She shook her head, but the sight of his light eyes glittering in the moonlight was doing strange things to her breathing. "Oh, Harry, you are so beautiful." She lifted trembling hands to trace his lips, his eyebrows, his firm proud jawline.

"Here, now. I am supposed to be seducing you!" Harrison closed the gap between them and brought his mouth down on hers gently, tenderly. He was determined not to frighten her off with too-passionate lovemaking.

It was a difficult vow to keep, for her lips softened under his, and she curved her body upward, straining toward him. She made a frustrated noise in her throat and removed her lips from his long enough to say, "If you are going to kiss me, then kiss me! As you did in your studio."

He smiled against her mouth. "You liked those kisses?"

"Is it compliments you want?" She balled her hand into a fist and hit him in the shoulder.

"Ah, Bella!" He kissed her as she wanted him to, hard and passionately. Her mouth opened eagerly to receive his tongue, and it was difficult to say who was panting the hardest when the need for air drove them apart.

"You drive me wild." Curzon folded her in his arms and kissed her again.

A burst of raucous laughter not far away reminded them of their whereabouts. Bella leaned away in his encircling arms. "We can't make love here." There was less concern for propriety than frustration in her voice.

Harrison chuckled low in his throat. *She is responding just as I hoped. Soon she will be mine.* "No, Bella, we can't. Which is just as well, for I've no wish to take my wife before her wedding night."

Bella gasped. "There won't be a wedding night, and you know it."

His hand slid around to cup her generous breast in his hand. Long slender fingers stroked her knowingly. "Yes, there will."

The fire Harrison Curzon had lit in her exploded at this intimate touch. "Oh, stop. No, don't stop. I . . ."

He kissed her again and again. His determination to lead her to the altar warred with the urge to take her there on the park bench. At last he pulled away, and turning her so that her back was to him, held her very close as he whispered in her ear.

"Isabella Eardley, hear me. I have fallen in love with you."

She stiffened. "No, Harry!"

"Yes, I have. I know I am supposed to be a rake, but do you know that I haven't been with a woman since that day in the studio. I don't want anyone but you."

Bella's heart fluttered in her chest. She had spent many hours reliving those kisses and caresses. She forced herself to respond coolly. "I am very flattered, of course, but I am not so naive as to believe that is love, Harry."

"It is more than just desire. I can't stand to see you being bored by the duke and beaten down into a poor tame creature by your relatives. I want to take you to wife. I want to see you flower into a strong, proud, accomplished woman."

Bella turned in his arms so she could look at him. She cupped her hand along his jaw. "I wish—"

"Harrison! Bella! Harrison! Bella! Where the devil are you?" Loud and anxious, the duke's voice carried from the main path.

On an oath, Curzon stood. "Why doesn't he just engage the watch to announce that I've wandered off with you. That idiot. Come along, Bella. We'll continue this conversation at another time. And I warn you—I will have my way!"

Bella let him take her hand and lead her away. She didn't feel like leaving. She felt like staying in his arms forever. *But my father and grandmother have put it beyond my power to be his wife, even if I did decide to marry him.* Bowed down by this realization, she paid little heed to the heated argument that ensued between the duke and Curzon before Winkham took her arm and led her back toward the brightly lit pavilion of Vauxhall.

"He has his nerve, lecturing me on propriety," Winkham groused.

"It wasn't exactly subtle of you, Winky. My reputation is doubtless in shreds. Why did you let him lead me off, anyway? You know his reputation. You also know my grandmother dislikes him intensely, for hasn't she lectured you several times on your attempts to pattern yourself after him?"

"If you must know, it was the wager! Come along. The fireworks are starting soon."

"Wager!" Bella dug in her heels, bringing them to a standstill. "Explain yourself."

"I, uh . . ." Suddenly aware he might have revealed too much, the duke looked everywhere but at Bella.

"Why, Winky, you are blushing! If I touched your cheek, I'm sure I would burn my finger."

"Tell you about it later. Please come along, Bella. I don't want to miss the display."

Bella stamped an imperious foot. "Tell me now, or take me straight home and forget your silly fireworks!"

Though she pretended great indignation when she had the truth out of the reluctant duke, Bella was secretly amused and charmed by Curzon's method of getting time alone with her. Part of her hoped he'd find other such occasions; part of her warned that such would be fatal to her mother's cause, not to mention her own wish to stay unwed!

Chapter Twelve

Harrison Curzon ignored the greetings called to him from various tables in Brooks's. There was only one person he wanted to see, and that was the Duke of Winkham. With grim purpose he strode through the gamblers until he came to a group of men concentrating on their cards.

"Winkham, I want to speak with you!"

The duke looked up, frowning. "Not now, Curzon. I'm busy."

"Now!" The tall blond leaned menacingly over the table, resting his hands on it to bring his face close to the duke's.

"I say, Harry! Take yourself off!" Arnold Lanscombe tried to remove one of the offending arms.

"Found yourself a sheep for the shearing, haven't you, Arnold. Never fear, I'll give him right back to you."

Realizing that Curzon intended to have his way, the duke stood. "Might as well. Luck's not with me anyway, tonight."

Once they were outside, Curzon set a pace difficult for the duke's shorter legs to match until they were well away from any listening ears. Then he turned menacingly on Winkham. "What's this rumor I hear, that you were seen kissing Bella, right on the lighted pathway near the pavilion last night."

"Not a rumor. Solid truth!"

"What do you mean to do, compromise her to make her marry you? I won't permit—"

The duke swelled with indignation. "Not what you think. When I got her in the light, saw her lips were swollen. Anyone would know she'd been kissed, and none too gently.

Better for the talk to be that I kissed her in full view of the world, than that either you or I had kissed her into that state in private."

"Oh!" Curzon tugged urgently at his ear. "I hadn't real-ized . . ." He silently cursed himself for his lack of self-control.

"What d'you mean, kissing her that way? Not how one treats a lady!"

"No, but it is how I treat my wife-to-be."

Winkham snapped his fingers into the taller man's face. "Told you! Her father wants a title for her. Daresay she wants it, too."

"And you will marry a woman who welcomes another man's kisses? Passionate kisses?"

Winkham looked petulant. "Did she? As to that, wel-comed mine, too. Told me so. Said she wanted more, so there!"

Curzon felt his hands clench into fists. "So! She's a bit of a wanton. I can see you've become a real man of the world, not to mind."

"I'll know how to keep her, once we're wed," Winkham declared. Curzon did not like the suddenly cruel set of the duke's mouth.

"Go back to your card game. Arnold Lanscombe has a fortune to recoup."

The duke saw the clenched fists and decided to make no rejoinder. He turned and scurried back to Brooks's, leaving Harrison Curzon standing with the taste of ashes in his mouth.

Considering the manner in which they parted, and his own decidedly hostile feelings against the Duke of Winkham, Curzon was startled to hear his butler announcing the man shortly after he returned from his morning painting session the next day.

"What do you want?" he growled.

"A bargain. I need your assistance."

Curzon stared at him. "Why should I help you?"

"Perhaps to have another opportunity to court Isabella?" The duke smiled slyly.

"Have a seat." Curzon sat also. He wanted an opportunity to talk to Bella, though thoughts of courting her were far from his mind. He meant to confront her with her behavior. *How dare she welcome the kisses of this obnoxious man. Or any man but me?*

"You were right about Lanscombe fleecing me. Others have, too. Enough that it's beginning to make serious inroads into my fortune. I want you to teach me the finer points of gambling. I've heard that you are an expert; indeed your winnings at all games of chance are legendary."

Curzon shook his head. "Not true. At games of chance I've lost almost as much as I've won. I rarely even play them anymore. I consider faro and E. O. the play of fools. No, I prefer games that involve skill."

"That makes sense, but I can't even win at whist. I find I don't like losing to men half my age. I may never be the whip that you are, but I want to be able to turn a card with the best of them."

Curzon studied the duke over templed fingers.

Taking encouragement from Curzon's silence, the duke tossed out his lure again. "Bella and I are going to spend the day at Richmond on Thursday. There is to be a picnic and boating at the Marquess of Penswold's estate. You invited?"

"Of course."

"Her parents and the duchess are going to accompany us, so you'd have no hope of getting near her without my help. One thing, though. No more kisses!"

"Since we have both endangered her reputation thereby, I must ask for the same pledge from you."

"Agreed." The duke stretched forward, offering his hand, which Curzon took forcefully. He launched upon his new duties immediately.

"Skill at whist means planning, foresight, and a good memory, in addition to knowing something of mathematical probabilities."

"I have an excellent memory, Curzon. Mathematics I must confess was my most difficult subject. Still, I will apply myself diligently." The duke's voice rang with boyish enthusiasm at odds with his years.

"No doubt," Curzon said dryly as he stood to get a new deck of cards. *What I do for you, Bella. Even while wondering if you are worth it!*

"I warn you, Winky, if you try any more of your sloppy kisses on me, I will slap your face." Bella pulled back against the duke's arm, trying to prevent him from drawing her away from the main path that led along the Penswolds' lakeshore.

"Not kisses, Bella. I've a debt to pay. Now come along." He tugged her up a small side path that wound into a spinney.

A debt to pay. Bella gave up her struggles, her heart beating faster. Had Harry won another chance to court her? *Oh, I wish I didn't want to see him so much! I don't want to love him!*

Curzon stepped out onto the path when they were well out of sight of the lake. His greeting was curt, and there was a tightness around his mouth that Bella had never seen before.

"Remember your promise, Curzon," the duke said as he turned abruptly back toward the lake.

"What promise?" Bella looked askance at the tall man looming over her. He looked decidedly angry.

"Never mind. Did you know London is buzzing with the news that you kissed the Duke of Winkham? Right in the public walkways of Vauxhall!"

He's jealous. Bella turned her eyes up flirtatiously. "You cannot tell me you are scandalized, now, can you? After all, you've been known to steal a kiss or two. I didn't know the *ton*'s little teapot tempests bothered you so much."

"When it concerns the woman I love, it does."

Bella's heart tripped over itself in response to this bald declaration, but she was determined that Curzon should not know the effect he had on her.

"Why are you looking so thunderously at me? Shouldn't you take it up with Winky? 'Twould be the cap on my season's success, to have a duel fought over me." She turned away, looking coyly back at him from the corners of her eyes.

Curzon turned her to face him squarely, his large hands cupping her shoulders. "Did you encourage his kiss, Bella? Did you like it, as he claimed?"

Isabella lifted her face to him. "Not as well as I liked yours, I think. Kiss me again and let me compare."

Curzon dropped his hands. "I am well served for my promiscuous life, aren't I? I've given my heart to a faithless wanton."

"No! That's not true." The look of pain on his handsome features cut her to the quick. She dropped her deliberately provoking behavior. "I hated his kiss. It was sloppy and disgusting. I don't want anyone to kiss me but you."

Suddenly she was in his arms, off her feet, and being held tightly against his chest. He buried his head in the hollow of her neck and shoulder. "Ah, Bella. I hope that is the truth. You are such a mendacious little minx!"

She thrust her arms around his neck and locked her hands. "It is true, Harry. I swear it! Now kiss me."

Reluctantly, Curzon released her, letting her slide down

his body, but keeping her close as her feet touched the ground. "I can't. I promised Winkham . . ."

"Don't I have any say? Really, the two of you treat me like chattel. I warn you, Harry, I won't be any man's property."

"I gave him my word that there would be no kisses if he helped me be private with you. Besides, we have a tendency to be carried past good sense when we kiss. I don't want to send you out of these woods with swollen lips as the duke says I did at Vauxhall the other night."

She touched her lips reminiscently. "It was lovely till he spoiled it."

"Why do you tolerate him? Don't tell me a resourceful female such as yourself can't find a way to give Winkham a disgust of you?" Light blue eyes looked at her demandingly.

She evaded his gaze. "It isn't as simple as you think." Her mother's anxious face flashed before her.

"He is convinced you will marry him. Says his title will weigh more than any feelings you might have for me. Is he right?"

"It weighs not at all with me, but my father is another matter. Oh, do leave off. I haven't changed my mind about marriage, Harry. I don't want to marry Winky, or you, or anyone else. At least . . ." Bella blushed. She was beginning to think her grandmother was right. Desire was a very powerful emotion! Right now she desired the kiss Harrison had denied her.

". . . at least not right away. Perhaps after a time."

Curzon studied her carefully, then traced her small straight nose with his index finger, sending a shock of sensation through her. "Not a very long time, I think." He cupped her face with his hand, stroking along her jawline and under her chin with his thumb.

Shivers of desire rushed through Bella. "You think to seduce me into marrying you!" She drew back indignantly.

A confident smile tilted one side of Curzon's mouth. "Perhaps."

"Your fifteen minutes are up." Winkham's strident voice interrupted Bella's response. "Come, Bella. your father saw me without you and is asking around. He's also noticed Harry isn't in sight. For some reason he positively loathes Harry." He held out his arm and led her away, leaving Curzon to grind his teeth in frustration.

"Here she is, sir. Told you she wasn't far away."

Bertram Eardley glared at his daughter. "Who were you with? And where? I am warning you, missy . . ."

Bella glanced at her mother's anxious face. "Father, there are some things you should not question a female too closely upon. Especially in mixed company." She turned her shoulder on him to take Winkham's arm. "I am thirsty, Winky. Take me to the refreshment tent."

Red-faced, Eardley watched them go. The duchess and Seraphina exchanged alarmed glances. She had not been in the ladies' withdrawing room as she implied. They had searched it immediately upon learning that Isabella wasn't with the duke.

"Ginny, how wonderful to see you." Bella slipped from Winkham's arm as they entered the refreshment tent, and ran to hug her friend. "Where is Gil?"

"We aren't joined at the hip," Virginia snapped.

Bella's eyebrows shot up at her friend's unusual display of bad temper.

Virginia flushed guiltily. "He's rowing Delilah Blessington around the lake. Lord Carrothers is bringing me some punch. Winky, why don't you do likewise for Bella?"

The girls watched the duke's retreating form in silence

for a moment before Ginny snickered. "Those pleated trousers make him look like a pear."

"He thinks they make him look like Harrison Curzon. Have you noticed how he copies Harry in everything."

"Who has not? It is so absurd. Everyone is laughing at him behind his back!" Ginny's own smile slid quickly from her lips.

"What is wrong, Ginny?"

Virginia's eyes filled with tears, which she rapidly blinked away. "I've faced the fact that I love Gilbert, but he still doesn't want to marry me. He's much more interested in Miss Blessington."

Bella laid her hand on the redhead's arm. "I'm sorry. Perhaps if you tried to make him jealous?"

"I am. I was, that is. I have been flirting with Stanley, but a few minutes ago Gil laughed at me. Says Stanley is devoted to a married woman, as well as being much too old for me."

"Stanley?"

"Lord Carrothers. Sssh, here they come."

She pasted on a bright smile for Lord Carrothers, which Bella copied for the duke, because her father had followed them and was now standing not far away, eyeing her suspiciously. *What a mendacious pair we are. Two of a kind, as Grandmama said!*

"So you are a follower of the fancy," Lord Carrothers was saying to Winkham as they approached the two young women.

"Certainly." The duke tried to look knowing the way Harrison Curzon did, with a slight curl to his lip. "Backed Tom Spring in his last fight. Knew he had a vicious left hook."

"True. He'd demonstrated it at Jackson's often enough. I collect you saw him box there."

The duke shook his head reluctantly. "Haven't managed to make my way there yet. So much to see and do in town, y'know. Do you . . . ?"

"I like to go a few rounds, yes. Your friend Curzon makes me a good sparring partner, though I wouldn't care to go up against him in a real fight."

Winkham preened himself at being counted a friend of Harrison Curzon's. "Naturally. Harry is good at everything he tries."

Carrothers winked at the girls. "Not quite. Can't shoot worth a darn."

Winkham brightened at that. "I'm an excellent shot. Manton himself said so."

Carrothers inclined his head. "Impressive!"

Bella swallowed a grin and reached for her glass of punch. "Thank you, Winky."

"Gilbert is a very good shot, too, Your Grace."

Winkham turned to Virginia. "Is he? We'll have to have a match sometime."

"If you do, I hope I will be able to see it!"

Carrothers studied Virginia's flushed, excited face for a moment and then shrugged. "Think I see a friend. Excuse me, ladies, Winkham." He bowed politely and walked away.

Bella shook her finger at Virginia. "You won't entrance another beau by bragging about your cousin, Ginny."

"I know. But it doesn't matter, for . . ." She noticed that Winkham was listening avidly. "Oh, do go away, Winky. Bella and I want to have a private coze."

"Yes, run along, Winky, do."

Resentfully, the duke gave them a curt bow and stalked away. He strolled over to join Isabella's father.

"You're a fine one to instruct me on attaching a beau. You won't leg-shackle the Duke of Winkham with such Turkish treatment, Bella."

"I should be so fortunate as to give him a disgust of me!"

"I knew it! You don't love him, even if you did kiss him at Vauxhall. Such a rare scandal, Bella. Do you know everyone is talking? Arnold Lanscombe bet Mabry Ventners that you'd be wed to the duke before the season is out. I asked Gil to place a wager for me against it. He wouldn't, of course. Said it wasn't the ladylike thing to do."

"Oh, Gil! Mister Propriety. You should set your cap for someone more interesting."

"He *is* interesting. Unfortunately, he's not interested in me! Oh, there's Harrison." She waved. "He's coming over."

Bella felt her heart race a little as she saw him approaching. He was looking at her in a most particular manner.

"I think he is still a little in love with me," Virginia exclaimed, believing Curzon's warm look was meant for her. She stepped forward to meet him, then simpered at him when he kissed her hand in his masterful fashion.

Bella bit her lip. She had no right to be jealous. After all, she didn't want him. *Liar! Right now you could pull Virginia's hair out. You're as jealous of him as he is of you.* Bella was rarely dishonest with herself, however willing she was to bend the truth to her own ends in dealing with obnoxious adults.

That night as she sat up late sketching from memory the lovely though artificial scenery of the Penswolds' estate, Bella pondered her problem. *Problems, actually. I can't, won't marry Winkham, yet what shall I do about my mother? I don't want to marry at all, yet I love Harry. He looked so hurt today when he thought I'd enjoyed Winky's kisses.*

It was her first taste of feminine power, but the power to wound another human being gave her no satisfaction. Rather, it gave her an unpleasant stab in the region of her heart to realize that if she continued to refuse Harrison Curzon he would be very hurt indeed. The third problem, of course, was herself. When she was near Harry, she forgot all about the need to dedicate herself to art. She wanted only to dedicate herself to loving him.

Chapter Thirteen

The room was filling rapidly. Harrison Curzon, standing at the back, talking with several acquaintances, was glad that Jean Maillot was holding a seat for him in the front row of the Royal Academy's assembly room.

"Amazing that Turner's lectures still draw such a good attendance, considering what they are," Thomas Priddington observed with a slight sneer.

"A great man is worth listening to no matter how poorly organized," Curzon responded in his most cutting tone. Priddington regarded himself as a qualified critic of the arts, on no better grounds than that he could afford to purchase what he wished. Curzon's eyes strayed to the door, where some sort of altercation was taking place.

He saw the porter, who had been checking the ivory admission tickets at the door, hustling a very small gentleman out of the room. Something about him seemed familiar.

"Excuse me, gentlemen. I see a friend." Curzon pushed through the crowd hastily. Outside the room he lengthened his stride and quickly caught up with the porter and the sputtering young man he was in the process of evicting from Somerset House.

"Hopper," he called.

"A moment, sir. I must eject this brash child. Tried to sneak in without a ticket, he did."

Curzon looked down into a familiar pair of vivid blue eyes. "Ah, just as I thought. It's young Clarence. What happened, cub. Did you lose the ticket I obtained for you?"

"No, sir. I quite forgot it in my excitement at attending the great Turner's lectures on perspective. I tried to explain to this . . . this . . ."

"Loyal and conscientious servant. Mr. Hopper, may I make known to you Monsieur Clarence de l'Imposteur, scion of an old French family, and eager student of myself and Mr. Maillot."

Mr. Hopper glared at the black-haired young man, but released his arm. "Why didn't ye say so, lad. I would have asked Mr. Curzon to vouch for you."

Without a moment's hesitation, the 'lad' responded, "I didn't know he was already inside."

"Come along, Clarence, we don't want to miss the first of the lecture." Curzon clapped his hand around the smaller man's shoulder and urged him forward. The porter touched his forehead respectfully.

Once inside the lecture hall again, Curzon steered his charge directly to the seat next to Maillot. There was no other seat nearby.

Upon seeing Curzon's companion, Maillot stood up. "The devil," he hissed through clenched teeth. "What mean you bringing that baggage here."

"Didn't bring him, but he's here, so perhaps you would consider lending him your seat. I see another near the back."

"Gladly." Maillot took up his notepad. "I want nothing to do with this prankster! If you are discovered smuggling a gently bred female into a Royal Academy lecture, I want to be as far away as possible!"

"Have a seat, Clarence." Curzon ran his eyes over her with amusement. "Unusual arrangement of your cravat. What do you call it?"

Isabella bent her head to study the neckcloth. "I was trying for a waterfall."

"More of a drip, I would say." He lowered his voice. "A very fashionable windswept, however, though black hair does not become you."

She dimpled. "It doesn't, does it. I look like death!"

"Shhh." Curzon bent near her ear to whisper, "I am no more eager than Maillot to have you discovered, and your voice is a dead giveaway. Do you think you can sit still for this? I warn you, Mr. Turner is famous for his ineptness as a lecturer."

"I don't care! I understand that tonight he will be discussing when to leave off rigid adherence to mathematical perspective in favor of an artist's vision of his subject."

Curzon nodded. "You are well informed."

Just then the famous artist entered the hall, followed by an assistant carrying a sheath of large drawings. Other drawings were already set up on easels both behind and in front of the elevated lectern.

Bella studied the little man with interest. *So that is J. M. W. Turner! He is as homely as his paintings are beautiful*, she thought. Her eyes swept the row of statuary in front of the lectern, some replicas, some originals of Greek and Roman sculpture. Hung on the wall behind the lectern was a large copy of *The Last Supper*. As Mr. Turner and his assistant were holding a whispered discussion of the arrangement of his lecture illustrations, Bella turned in her chair to examine the rest of the room.

She felt a swell of pride as she realized that two of Mary Moser's paintings flanked the fireplace, and Angelica Kaufman's work decorated the ceiling. *How can anyone deny me the right to study art*, she wondered, *when the Academy itself is filled with the work of women?* Harrison's voice whispering in her ear recalled her to reality.

"Turn back around, Monsieur l'Imposteur. I don't want too many of my colleagues to get a clear look at that radiant face. Even with black hair, you make a very *pretty* young man."

Bella noticed then for the first time that she was the only female in the room, gently bred or otherwise. The sea of masculine faces suddenly seemed menacing to her. She turned around hastily, glad that Curzon was beside her. She took up her notepad and nervously began sketching in the margins. When Turner began lecturing, she took copious notes, though his voice was so low it was difficult for her to hear him even from the front row.

After the lecture Curzon advised that they hold back, examining the illustrations, until most of the men had left the room, to prevent penetration of her disguise.

"I had hoped to meet Mr. Turner." She started toward the small man, surrounded now by well-wishers. "Mayn't we—"

"That you will not do, Monsieur Clarence!" Curzon clapped his hand firmly on her elbow. "Turner is no fool. I could lose all credit with him and my other artist colleagues, were your identity to be discovered. Acceptance by them was too dearly won for me to give it up carelessly."

Though disappointed, Bella understood. She turned aside to study Turner's intricate painting of the interior of Brocklesby Mausoleum. "Did he do this just for his lectures? It is magnificent."

"This and hundreds more. He may not be much to listen to, but he has certainly done a valiant job of preparing. What did you think of the lecture? Could you make head or tail of it?"

"Of course!" She tilted her chin up defensively. "And I agree with him entirely. We are artists, not mathematicians or architects. We need to know the rules of perspective, but we can't be bound by them!"

He soundlessly clapped his hands. "Brava, little tigress. I thought you would feel that way."

The look of understanding that passed between them kindled a deeper, more arousing emotion in Curzon. He looked around him cautiously. This was not the time or place for intimate glances. "I think we can safely leave now, and then you have some explaining to do."

He led her to his carriage, which was standing outside Somerset House. Though the night was warm, a light drizzle had set in, and the carriage lamps were reflected in small puddles on the street.

"Oh! Mr. Maillot." Isabella hesitated as she entered, upon discovering the irascible artist already seated in the carriage.

"Damn you, Harry. Why did you not send her to the right about! I'll walk!" He started for the other door.

"Stay, Jean. You'll get soaked." Harrison nudged Bella up the steps and followed her in.

"Better soaked than ruined!" The carriage rocked as the other man stepped hastily out and slammed the door.

"He hates me."

"No, he fears you. And not without reason. You saw how your grandmother treated him that day in the studio."

Bella sighed and sank back against the squabs. "She can be dreadfully autocratic at times."

"Now I wish my curiosity satisfied. How did you get here?"

"I took a hackney cab, of course. You surely don't think I walked in the dark."

Curzon fought to control his exasperation. "Keep talking. How did you escape your guardians?" And those clothes, that wig . . ."

She grinned and plucked proudly at the man's jacket she was wearing. "I sold a perfectly hideous pearl and garnet necklace. Grandmama locked my jewelry box, but left it in my room, not knowing that I have never yet been defeated by a lock! I ordered them using Clarence's measurements and told the tailor they were a present for my younger brother. It is a more successful disguise than the page's uniform, don't you think?"

"In most respects. Your derriere still looks temptingly female."

She dipped her head to avoid his deliberate leer. "I tried padding there, but everything I did looked so unnatural, I finally gave up."

Curzon reached out and lifted off the wig.

"Ow! It's pinned." Bella slid her hand under the wig and deftly freed it from her head. "Oh, that feels much better! How uncomfortable that thing is!"

He ruffled his hands through her tousled golden curls. "Mmmm. Much better." He leaned down.

She drew away. "Now, Harrison. You mustn't. I didn't sneak out for you to seduce me."

"Still, we might as well make use of the opportunity." He put his arm around her and drew her firmly into his lap.

"I mean it!" She slid away. "I must be getting back. My grandmother and mother will not stay at the Panshawes' rout very late."

"How did you get them to leave you behind?"

"For two days I have been complaining of the toothache. Grandmama said I must have it pulled if it was still paining me tomorrow. However, I think this evening's rest and the dose of laudanum she left me will put it all to rights." Even in the dimly lit carriage her eyes sparkled with mischief.

Curzon chuckled. "You are a complete hand, Bella. None of your servants saw you leave? Or have you managed to suborn another one?"

She shook her head vehemently. "I wouldn't wish to be responsible for anyone else losing their place. No, I climbed down the roof drains."

Curzon sat up straight. "You . . . My God, Bella! You could have been killed."

She shook her head. "I am very agile. I used to climb trees like a boy until they put me in corsets and silly girl's slippers. It was easy as can be!"

Harry folded his arms on his chest and glared at her. "And just how do you propose to get back in?"

"The same way, of course."

"You most certainly will not! I could never bear to watch that. Besides, it is raining now. Everything will be slick. I collect it was not raining when you left?"

Bella frowned. "I hadn't thought of that!"

Curzon gathered her into his arms. "I think I will just keep you. They'll have to let me marry you if you spend the night with me." Without waiting for her to reply, he kissed her.

I am drowning! Bella clutched Harrison's lapels tightly. *I must stop him!* But she could not seem to do anything but kiss him back.

He took her on his lap once again. Sliding his hand inside her coat and vest, he cupped one full breast gently. "Say you'll stay, Bella."

"Harry! What are you doing to me?" Suddenly boneless, she melted in his arms.

"You'll stay." He chuckled.

"No! I . . . I can't. Oh, Harry, there is more to my situation than you can understand. Besides—"

"I know. You don't want to marry." Curzon's low growl was resentful.

Bella pulled away a little to explain. "Perhaps I will change my mind later, but not now." She added slyly, "After all, I am very young."

He sighed. "Yes, you are, minx, but you have an old soul. Ah, well, I can wait until you are ripe, but don't let anyone else pick you from the tree. That jackanapes Winkham seems to think you will marry him. I won't stand for it!" As he whispered against her ear, Curzon continued to caress her so that she could barely think.

"I won't. But until the very end of the season I have to let the duke court me, have to let them think I might accept him. Oh, Harry, please!"

"Please stop, or please continue?" His teeth flashed in a knowing grin.

"Both!"

They both started laughing. He removed his hand from her clothing and cuddled her close as their laughter wove stronger, deeper strands around his heart, binding him to her in a way he had never thought to know. Her petiteness made him want to protect her, at the same time that her valiant spirit filled him with admiration. *I don't want to take her without her complete consent*, he realized. *I could seduce her, but I want her to be mine in soul as well as body.*

They sat together silently for a time after the laughter faded. At last he sighed. "You're sure you want to go back?"

"I must."

He frowned. "Well, you damn sure aren't climbing up the drains! I'll have to think of some way to get you in the house." He opened the panel and called Bella's address out to his driver.

In the duchess's garden Curzon stared up the drains that had been Isabella's path to freedom, ice water filling his veins. "Bella!" He grabbed her shoulders and shook her. "You are never to do that again, do you hear me! Never. And I don't want you wandering the streets of London at night, either. *I* am not entirely safe all alone, much less you. Do you suppose no one will attack you because you are dressed as a male?"

She looked up at him with a mulish expression. "I want to hear the next lecture!"

Curzon shook his head. "Too risky. Promise me—"

"No! I won't. I don't want to lie to you."

"Bella! You mustn't—"

"I thought you understood that I must study art! That

means more than just sitting in my studio, dabbing paint on canvas."

Curzon gritted his teeth and looked at the stubborn, determined miss. "Would it help if I brought you my notes on his lectures? I've attended the full course twice. I venture to say that my notes are clearer than his lectures. You'd miss the illustrations, of course, but—"

Bella beamed. "Would you? I could copy them!"

She is as excited as any of my mistresses have been upon receiving a diamond necklace, Curzon thought. He traced her radiant smile with his forefinger.

"If I give them to you, you will promise me not to climb down the drain pipe again?"

She hesitated, studying his anxious face. At last she lifted a soothing hand and drew it along his jawline. "Poor Harry. You are really, truly worried about me aren't you."

"I know that the very young think that they are immortal. I did when I was your age and for far too long afterward. But it isn't true, Bella."

She smiled tenderly at him. "I will promise you. How will you get the lectures to me?"

"We should both give that some thought. You will be at the Ramswoods' ball, I assume."

She nodded.

"We will discuss it then. Now I had best get you inside before your family returns and finds you missing."

"And then he banged on the kitchen door and pretended to be drunk. When Bridey, who sleeps in front of the fire, came to the door he told her he had dropped a purse of gold and the coins had scattered. He was weaving and slurring his words. It was such a good performance, he could go upon the boards. You won't be surprised to learn that Bridey hastened into the darkness to search for them. I expect he was one or two coins short when they were all gathered up."

"And you sneaked in while she was searching!" Virginia clapped her hands together gleefully, then glanced around the crowded ballroom to see if anyone had noticed.

"Mrs. Filmore gave me quite a scare. She came out of her apartment to see what the commotion was. I had to shrink back into the pantry. But I made it up the servants' stairs. I had barely changed into my nightrail when my mother came in to check on me."

"How I admire your courage. But I agree with Harrison. What you did was very dangerous, Bella."

Bella bit her bottom lip. "I know. Harry read me a proper scold and made me promise not to do it again."

The two young women sat silent for a few minutes. Bella gradually realized that there was an aura of suppressed excitement about Virginia.

"You are looking like the cat that ate the cream, Ginny. What is up with you?"

Virginia blushed and looked self-consciously at her hands. "Does it show?"

"Tell me! Tell me! It's something to do with Gilbert, isn't it?"

Ginny lifted joy-filled eyes to Bella. "Oh, Bella, you mustn't tell anyone, but he has proposed. We are to announce our engagement as soon as my father returns from France."

Bella leaned over to embrace her friend. "I am so happy for you. How did it come about?"

"Lord Carrothers proposed."

"What?"

"Yes, and my mother was all for my accepting him. Gilbert was beside himself, said he wouldn't permit it. I resented his high-handed tone, and we fell into one of our usual rows. All of a sudden he blurted out, 'I know you don't care a pin for me, Ginny, but I love you, and I'll not see you married to a man whose heart lies elsewhere, who marries only for an heir.' Well, I was so bowled over I began to cry, and he took me into his arms to comfort me, and we kissed and . . . oh! It was wonderful! He has loved me all along, can you imagine! He never let on, because I fussed so about the engagement. When I told him I had objected primarily because I thought he didn't love me, he was so incensed we almost began another row! I expect we'll quarrel all of our lives, but I never guessed making up could be so much fun."

Bella suppressed a strong twinge of jealousy. She could well imagine how delightful making up with Harrison Curzon would be. "It is of all things wonderful!"

"Yes, now I don't have to spend the rest of the season in jealousy, or terror that someone my mother thinks thoroughly acceptable will offer for me."

"As I do. A certain odious and determined someone! Oh, there is Harrison. We must discuss how to get his Turner notes to me. Quick! You must distract my partner. Harry shall have this waltz!"

Chapter Fourteen

"It's Mr. Lamposter, isn't it?" The Royal Academy's porter peered into the young man's face questioningly.

"You remember me!"

"I never forget a face, young sir. Be you seeking Mr. Curzon?"

He is the last person I want to see, Bella thought, but she smiled and nodded her head at the porter.

"He is in the life drawing class."

"You needn't show me to it; just point the way."

The porter shook his head. "Don't know about that. Not supposed to have visitors in the life classes. Still, the model is male today. I think there could be no harm in letting you go up. Now if t'were a female . . ."

"I'd have no hope, more's the pity!" Bella tried for the knowing grin of a healthy young male.

"Right you are, youngster. The Academy is most particular who is admitted when a female model is posing. Can't have any lascivious behavior, now, can we?"

"Which way, then?"

The porter gave her directions and she scampered up the steps, her small drawing pad clutched to her side. *A male model! What luck!*

She entered the studio as quietly as possible. The room was filled with earnest men standing at easels, drawing. *I will not, must not blush*, Bella warned herself as she spotted the healthy nude male standing on the raised platform in the position of a discus thrower at the back of his swing.

One or two heads raised up as she entered the room, but none challenged her. Curzon's blond head was bent over his sketch in deep concentration. She slid into place at the only vacant easel in the room and propped up her tiny drawing pad on it. She had come intending to sneak into the sculpture gallery to do some studies of the statues, but this opportunity to draw the male form from life was just too tempting to pass up.

She quickly forgot her embarrassment. Lost to the world as she drew rapidly, she almost knocked over the easel, so startled was she at the indignant male voice whispering harshly in her ear.

"What are you doing at my easel? This is *my* easel." A thin, pinch-faced young man stood over her, glaring indignantly.

"I beg your pardon, sir." She grabbed her sketch pad and stepped away. The young man who confronted her was not so easily placated, though.

"You are not an academy member!" His voice rose, jarring several of the other artists out of their absorption with their task. "What are you doing here? No one is allowed in here but members, and over the age of twenty-one at that! And you are not either, unless I miss my guess!" He reached for her drawing pad. His fingers were closing on it when a familiar deep voice sounded from behind Isabella.

"Ah, young Clarence, is it? Looking for me, cub? Mr. Hopper should have come for me, though, instead of letting you in here. It is as Mr. Henley says. You are not permitted in the life classes."

Bella tugged her sketch pad free of Mr. Henley's fingers. "I am sorry, sir. I didn't know. The porter said it would be acceptable for me to come in since it was a *male* model. . . ." She dared a look into Curzon's face. To her relief, he looked more amused than angry. His tolerance, however, did not extend to abetting her when she tried to stay to complete her sketch.

"I think not. Mr. Henley, we'll keep you from your

drawing no longer. Come with me, Clarence." He took Bella's elbow and hustled her out of the room.

Once in the hall, he glared down at her. "Are you trying to get me expelled from the membership? And you promised me you wouldn't do this anymore."

"I promised you I wouldn't climb down the drainpipe again, and I didn't. I changed clothes at Madame de Coursey's while supposedly trying on a gown, and then sneaked out the back. My grandmother had gone next door to check upon some gloves she had ordered."

"Have you no pity, Bella? She is probably frantic with worry about you."

"If you knew how they are treating me, you would realize they don't deserve any consideration at all! Anyway, I left her a note telling her I had to get away by myself a little to think. Let her worry. Let them all worry. Perhaps they'll stop trying to force me into their mold!"

" 'La belle dame sans merci'."

Bella tossed her head. "As I said, when they show me mercy, then I will return the favor. Oh, Harry, it is fascinating to be able to walk the city without chaperonage or fear of being molested. I've almost a full sketchpad of drawings I made of all kinds of people and places I would ordinarily never see." She held it up to him eagerly.

Curzon groaned. How could he explain to her that beautiful young boys stood in almost as much danger of being molested as young girls. "I will look at it later. First we must get out of here."

"Don't you want to finish your drawing?"

"What I want to do and what I am going to do are two different things."

The porter greeted them cheerily as they passed his station. "Good day, Mr. Curzon, Mr. Lamposter."

"Mr. Lamposter?" Curzon's brow knitted.

"I think that is his version of L'Imposteur. Fortunately for me, the man knows no French."

He grinned. "I was counting on it when I introduced you as such. I *wasn't* counting on your showing up in the life drawing class."

"I'm sorry about that, truly." Bella tried her best to look contrite. "I meant to sketch the statuary, but when Mr. Hopper offered to let me in there, I just couldn't resist."

Curzon shook his head. "Don't come the repentant sinner on me, Bella. I know you too well."

Once they were outside Somerset House, blinking in the bright afternoon light, Curzon took her sketch pad and flipped through it while they went in search of a hackney cab, since he had walked from his home on Cavendish Square.

Bella studied his face anxiously. "Are they any good?"

He sucked on his lower lip as he flipped the pages. "Most of them are very good, as I am sure you know. I can see you've been studying the notes on perspective."

"Oh, yes! Thank you so much for leaving them in the garden!"

At the sudden dark scowl on Curzon's face she stood on tiptoe to see which of her drawings had drawn his disapproval. It was her sketch of the live model.

"Did you have to go into such detail! And you seem to have concentrated your efforts on a particular part of his anatomy."

Bella flushed, but answered firmly. "Yes! When was I apt to see such again? I had to get it all down."

"Tell me, Bella, when do you expect to be using this knowledge in your work? Are you going to set up as a pornographer?" Curzon's eyes flashed with anger.

"I expect you have never accurately drawn the female figure, then!" She looked up at him defiantly.

He drew in a deep indignant breath, and then burst out laughing. "Oh, very well. I have. I expect there are some things artists draw for themselves alone."

"Just to see if they can." She nodded her head. "My interest is not prurient, I assure you."

He flicked her nose with his forefinger. "See that it isn't. I think I am more jealous than shocked."

Relief flooded her. "You haven't the least reason to be jealous."

"Hmmm. I'm not sure exactly how to take that!" He motioned her into a cab. "How shall we smuggle you back in?"

"I left my bundle of clothes with a flower girl. I think she was that very one you portrayed in your painting. I gave her some coins to keep the clothes for me."

Curzon gave the flower girl's address to the cab driver and then took Bella's hand. "So far your sense of adventure has not done you any harm, but I must explain a few home truths to you, at the risk of making you think I am no better than your strict grandmother."

He did not pull his punches in explaining what could happen to one so young and attractive, whether male or female, walking about unprotected on London's busy streets. When he had finished, her face was pale and she was shaking.

"I never imagined . . ."

"No, how should you? Bella, marry me. We'll run away if your family won't accept my proposal. I will see that you have the opportunity to observe the world in safety."

She seems almost convinced. Bella's eyes were huge and solemn in her face as she thought over his offer. Curzon resisted the impulse to pull her into his arms and use his love-making to persuade her.

"I . . . I . . . will think about it."

"Bella!"

"There is a reason I can't agree just yet."

"Which is?"

"I can't tell you."

"This is the second time today you've hinted at some mystery. Can you not confide in me? Let me help you."

She looked at her hands, twisting the expensive masculine gloves nervously. "Not yet. I am hoping to find a solution on my own. You see, if I do marry you, I don't want you to despise my . . . family."

He frowned. "I think I already do!"

She turned her head away.

"No, I didn't mean it, Bella. I'll love whomever you love, if it kills me."

"Oh, Harry!" She threw herself into his arms just as the hackney stopped in front of the flower stand.

Darting an anxious look to see if anyone had observed a young boy embracing him passionately, Curzon pulled her arms from around his neck. "Not now! Dressed like that, you could get me hanged." He opened the door, motioning her out. "I don't suppose you've given any thought to where you'll change?"

"In the cab, of course!"

Curzon's eyebrows rose. "Can I watch?" His eyes gleamed with mischief and desire. Bella felt her heart begin to race and her body to flush with warmth. Pretending to ignore him, she greeted the flower girl and retrieved her bundle. Curzon tossed the young woman an additional handful of coins before rejoining Bella in the cab.

"No, you must get out here. I'll change as the cab takes me to Hyde Park. I can walk home from there."

"Unaccompanied? Hasn't anything I've said made an impression on you."

"Oh!"

"I'll shut my eyes while you change and then deliver you directly to your street and watch while you go into Carminster House." He drew the curtains on the cab and folded his arms, matching her mulish look with one of his own.

"Oh, very well!"

"Stop that crying, Seraphina," Bertram Eardley snarled at his wife, who shrank against the cushions of the duchess's sofa as he shook his fist at her.

"Bertram, I'll thank you to remember your word to me," the duchess ground out through clenched teeth.

"My word is as good as yours. See her married into the *ton*, will you? Not bloody likely, with her disappearing from dress shops and returning hours later, refusing to account for her whereabouts. And with the drawing of a nude male! My God, what are you, Bella?"

"An artist." Bella thrust her chin out. "A very good artist!"

"You won't be such a good artist after I've finished breaking your hands, which I will do if you ever repeat this afternoon's performance." Eardley stood and crossed to where his daughter sat perched on a Sheraton chair. He yanked her up and shook her savagely.

Seraphina screamed. The duchess pushed herself up, using her cane.

"Stop that. Stop it at once."

He paid her no mind. Bella's head slammed back and forth.

"You'll injure her. Stop it!"

"I'll bloody well kill her! Ow! Ow!" He let go of his daughter to shield his own head as the duchess rained blows down on it with her cane.

The two antagonists confronted one another. For a moment it looked as if Eardley would strike the duchess, but her imperious look won out. He stepped back and snarled at her, "If you are to have your precious daughter back, you'd better see that Bella accepts Winkham. No more delays!

Now, before she has ruined herself and can't get a street sweeper to marry her."

Bella stormed, "You promised me I could wait until the end of the season."

"Your season is over! You will begin selecting your trousseau and planning a wedding. A duchess, my girl, and you should damn well be glad of it."

"Well, I'm not. I don't like him. He is stupid and self-centered and—"

"Sit down, Bella." The duchess's icy voice cut across their argument. "For once we are in agreement, Bertram. Bella, this very night you will give the duke the encouragement he needs to make his offer."

"I won't!"

"You will," her father declared, "or I will take you and your mother back to Hertfordshire with me and deal with both of you there."

"You are despicable to threaten my mother as a means of forcing me to wed a man I don't love."

"You'll thank me for it someday! Besides, I've been invited to hunt with the Quorn as the result of your association with the duke. I will allow nothing and no one to prevent it."

Bella's full mouth twisted into a bitter sneer. "You care less for your wife and daughter than for a pack of hounds."

Eardley lashed out at her, catching her sharply across the cheek with his open palm. "Shut up, you baggage!"

The blow knocked Bella back into her chair, tears of pain gushing from her eyes.

The duchess grabbed her son-in-law's arm. "You are not only a vicious brute, but a fool, Bertram Eardley. Thanks to you, she won't be able to show her face to anyone for days, much less accept the duke's proposal. Think you he will want a bride that has been beaten into accepting him?"

He looked at the hand-shaped red welt on Bella's fair skin and swore. "As soon as she is able, she will accept him, and never let him guess she is not delighted to do so, or else!"

The only sound in the room for several moments after Eardley stormed out was that of Seraphina's quiet weeping.

Bella explored her cheek with a shaking hand, then rubbed the back of her neck, which felt as if it were broken. Her head was spinning.

The duchess stroked her head with a cool, soft hand. "Poor child. I pray God he did not injure you."

Bella did not reply. She was looking at her mother, weeping helplessly on the sofa. She remembered the night at the opera last week, when Seraphina had sparkled with happiness. Filled out and with the anxious lines erased from her face, she had appeared almost pretty. Until today Bella had never felt the full force of her father's brutality. Now she truly understood the terror both she and her mother faced if she refused to marry the duke.

"Bella." The duchess bent to look her in the eye, a hand resting on each shoulder. "You must marry the duke. You do see that?"

"Isn't there some other way? I don't love the duke."

"Many of us have made a good life with a man we do not love."

"You did not love grandfather?"

"Once I did—before he sacrificed my children for money."

"Now you are sacrificing me!"

The duchess straightened. Leaning heavily on her cane, she went to the window that looked out on the street. "It isn't the same thing. If I don't convince you to marry Winkham, what will your father do to you? Marry you to one of his aging roué friends, no doubt. You have to marry. This foolishness about remaining unwed! Sooner or later you would disgrace us all. Though I make no doubt you'll end up in disgrace anyway, given your hey-go-mad behavior, I hope to see you safely married first. And it isn't as if you love someone else."

"But I do!"

Seraphina gasped. The duchess turned her head to glare at Bella. "How could you? You've never shown the least partiality to anyone."

"I love Harrison Curzon."

Her grandmother laughed. "You hardly know the man."

"I know him much better than you think."

"What does that mean?" The duchess faced her, an ominous look on her face.

"I have danced with him—"

"Very seldom, and then only because that fool Winkham lost sight of you."

"I have been to his studio."

"Suitably chaperoned, or so you said."

"I've been there since. Twice. We very nearly made love there."

"That proves nothing except that he deserves his reputation as a rake."

"If he was a rake, he had the opportunity then to take advantage of me. He didn't. When I asked him to stop kissing me, he did. Immediately. And twice since then I have been completely in his power and he has been a gentleman. He loves me."

"Twice! Blessed Heavens, did anyone see you?" The duchess visibly shuddered.

"Mama, the Curzons are very good *ton*, and very rich," Seraphina said. "Perhaps Bertram would consider—"

"Rot! Bertram wants his daughter to marry into one of the titled families. He's found one of the few where he would be a welcome in-law. I can just see Sir Randall Curzon welcoming such as him! They almost came to blows at the Curzons' ball."

"Oh, Bella. Do you truly love him?" Seraphina sadly scanned her daughter's face.

"Seraphina, don't encourage her. Harrison Curzon is a womanizer, unfit for marriage."

Bella slipped off her chair and knelt at her mother's side. "Yes, I do, Mama. And I am sure that if you would stand up to Father the way Grandmama did today, he could be made to see reason."

The duchess made a rude noise. "Bertram has no legal right to abuse me. There are few restrictions on what he may do to you and Seraphina short of killing you. If you love your mother, if you have a care to your own happiness, you will accept the duke. That is the long and the short of it. You must face the facts."

Bella looked from her mother's tear-streaked face to the duchess's grim one. Slowly, sadly, she slid up into the seat by her mother and hugged her. "Don't be so afraid, Mother. I won't abandon you to him. I will do what I must."

Chapter Fifteen

Harrison Curzon passed through the receiving line at the Stantons' ball with the most perfunctory of civilities. His stern features were enough to make acquaintances turn away rather than greet him. Ice blue eyes scanned the ballroom with grim purpose. When he spotted his prey, he circled the room with impolite haste. The second the country dance ended, he was on the floor by Bella's side.

""Why, Mr. Curzon. You gave me quite a start!"

"The next dance is mine, I think."

"Now wait a moment," Sir Ralph Moreton protested. "First the promenade, and then I must take her back to her chaperone."

"Ummm." Isabella pretended to study her dance card. "That's right, Harry. You're next. Don't be tedious, Sir Ralph." Mortally insulted, Moreton bowed curtly to her and stomped from the floor.

Curzon offered her his arm. *He's got that grim look about the mouth again*, Bella thought, bracing herself for a much-deserved scold as she allowed herself to be led off the floor by this obviously furious man. She did not hold back when he steered her through the French doors and onto the terrace.

"We haven't long, Harry. My father is watching me like a hawk. I know you must wonder—"

"Damn right I do. 'I never want to marry, Harrison.' and then, 'I am very young; I need time, Harrison.' 'I love you, Harrison.' 'I won't marry the duke, Harrison.' And then this morning I find your engagement announcement in the papers. The wedding to be in St. George's in a week."

Bella unfurled her fan. The warmth of the night was affecting her less than the fiery blast of his anger. "I can explain—"

"Is it true? That is all I want to know. Is it true? I want to hear it from your own lips."

"Yes, but—"

"You were forced into it, weren't you? Only say the word, Bella, and I will see that Winkham withdraws his offer."

How would he do that? Bella wondered. *Force a duel on Winky?* A shiver of apprehension ran up her spine at this very masculine solution to her dilemma. The duke was an excellent shot, as was her father. Harry was not. She was not about to sacrifice Harry's life for her mother, and that could well be the result if she explained to him while he was in this mood. She stared wordlessly up at the man she loved, trying to think what to say to him.

"There you are, Bella. The duke and I were wondering where you had gotten to."

Bella jumped at the sound of that familiar, strident voice. "Father! Winky! It was so hot in the ballroom, we were just taking the air, but it is even hotter out here." She fanned herself frantically.

"I would have taken you out for air, Bella. Ain't right you should come outside with anyone else than your fiancé." Winkham insinuated himself between Bella and Curzon.

"Well, Harry, ain't you going to wish us happy? You must have heard of our engagement." He grinned triumphantly.

"I asked Bella a question. I am waiting on her answer before I wish anyone anything."

Three pairs of eyes stared at Bella. She lifted her chin and met Harrison's icy gaze unwaveringly. "No, Mr. Curzon. I do not require your assistance. I am quite able to manage my own affairs."

Winkham grinned triumphantly up at Curzon. "There, that's landed you a facer. Come, my love. I have been looking forward to this waltz all evening."

Curzon watched them walk away, his teeth clenched. Bertram Eardley remained, feet spread wide and jaw jutting pugnaciously. "What do you mean, luring my gel out here alone?"

Curzon slowly, deliberately scanned the terrace. There were upwards of a half-dozen couples strolling about, talking in low voices. He looked back at Eardley and raised one eyebrow. "Alone?"

"Stay away from her. She is engaged. I mean to see her wed to Winkham before the week is out!"

"Since Bella has indicated her willingness, that is no concern of mine, Mr. Eardley. I bid you good evening!" Curzon did not return to the house, but exited the garden through the back gate that led to the mews.

As Bella and Winkham moved into the light spilling from the ballroom, the duke stopped abruptly. "Here, now. Why are you looking like a tragedy queen? Not regretting our engagement, are you?"

Bella swallowed hard. "No, Winky, of course not."

"Because if you are . . . Bertie assured me you were not being forced. I won't have that, Bella! I'm a duke, after all. Lots of females hovering around me." He thrust out his chest proudly.

Mendacity had never come harder to Bella, but she forced a smile to her face. "Don't be silly, Winky. I am only sorry that I had to hurt Harrison's feelings, that is all."

The duke laughed. "Never mind. Harrison Curzon won't wear the willow long! We'll all be great friends, you'll see."

* * *

The sound of hammering drew Jean Maillot upstairs to Harrison's studio. The door was open, and inside Harry wielded a hammer on a packing crate. Many of the paintings that had been hung or propped along the studio walls were stacked neatly according to size.

"What the devil is going on, Harry? You're making enough noise to raise the dead, and at the ungodly hour of nine A.M. at that."

Barely glancing at him, Harrison left off his task to walk over to the armoir, where he yanked out an armful of silks and feathers. "Here. You may as well have these props. I won't be needing them anymore."

Maillot caught part of the bundle. The rest slithered to the floor in a colorful pool around his feet.

"And why not? Are you letting that faithless little minx get to you? Why should you give up your art because of her engagement? She isn't worth it."

"No, she isn't, but somehow this studio has become permeated with memories of her. Besides, I won't have time anymore. I'm going into politics, remember. M'father wants me to stand in a bye-election."

Maillot watched Harry pull another armload of costumes from the cabinet. "I don't need those, Harry. I paint landscapes, remember?"

"Just so. Well, I shall send them to Drury Lane. They can add them to their stage properties."

Jean shook his head. "I knew I was wasting my time, teaching you. Art is not a high enough calling for a gentleman, after all." He spun on his heel and stalked out of the room.

Dropping another load of clothes onto the floor, Curzon swore softly under his breath. *It seems no matter what I do, I must disappoint someone.*

Moodily, he walked over to the painting of Isabella and Virginia, which still stood on a large easel. It was all but complete. He had never quite managed to capture the expression of determination on Bella's face while at the same time portraying her youthful beauty. Each time he tried, he ended up making her look hard, or older than she was. *Perhaps that is how it should look. She is hard! She looks soft and sweet but she has no heart.*

Mixing paint swiftly on his palette, he took up his brush and began reworking Isabella's features one more time. Stepping back, he saw immediately that he had failed again. He threw the brush he was holding at the painting. It landed with a splash in the middle of the canvas, and slid down trailing ivory paint through the center.

No matter. I don't want it anyway, and don't want anyone else to have it. I'll just burn it. Curzon began cleaning his brushes.

Bella waited until the first traces of light picked out the shape of the town house next to her grandmother's. After what Harry had told her that day about the kinds of evil lurking on the streets of London, she had no wish to be about while it was still dark.

She had arrived home from the ball at two A.M. Her father had stood outside her door while her maid helped her undress, and then locked her in her room, as he had been doing since the fateful day that she came home from Somerset House with the sketch of the nude discus thrower. Unlike her grandmother, her father knew of her knack for picking locks, so he also had taken the precaution of posting a footman outside her door at night.

Bella yawned mightily. She had been unable to sleep. She kept seeing Harry's pinched, angry face, the flash of pain in his eyes as she told him she didn't need his help. *I can't just leave it at that*, she thought. *Even if I have to go through with the marriage, he mustn't think it is for lack of caring for him.*

The sky was barely light. *Would there be many people on the streets?* Bella shuddered at the thought that she might encounter the sort that Harry had described to her. She hated the thought of walking all the way to his studio after learning of the seamier side of London life, but she had no choice. Her father had taken every last coin of hers, and even her jewelry box. Of course, the young man's suit had been confiscated.

But he didn't know about the page's uniform, she thought with satisfaction. She had always enjoyed outwitting her father, but never more so than today. Climbing down the drainpipe, she felt hardly a twinge of guilt for breaking her promise to Harry. Instead, she felt triumph over the tyrant who had thought to shut her away from the man she loved.

She was hungry. She had been too upset to partake of supper last night at the dance. Leaving by the drainpipes, she had no opportunity to nip a roll or bit of cheese from the kitchen. *Surely Harry will have something to eat in his studio*, she thought yearningly as she passed stalls where street merchants were beginning to set up their wares. The scent of fried pies tormented her.

At last, tired and trembling from a combination of fear and hunger, she stealthily climbed the three steps to the front door of the building that housed Harrison's studio. She did not want to alert the porter. She wanted to give Harrison no opportunity to refuse to see her. She could only hope that Harry would follow his usual pattern and come to his studio this morning.

Unfortunately, her soft footfalls brought Jean Maillot to the door of his parlor. He folded his arms and glared at her furiously. "Go home, selfish little cat. You have done enough harm."

Bella wasn't surprised to be the recipient of Maillot's anger. Without replying, she marched past him, chin held high, and mounted the stairs. Surprised to find the door to Harry's studio open, she entered the studio. *He's here!* Harry had his back to her and was vigorously cleaning his brushes. In front of him stood the painting that he had begun—it seemed so long ago—while she and Virginia were visiting his studio.

She stood for a long time staring at the painting of herself and Virginia. The sight of the ivory splatter and the long streak trailing from it down the center of the canvas startled her. Why had he damaged such an interesting painting?

He did a wonderful job of catching Ginny's coloring, she thought. *But as for his treatment of me!* Pain lanced through her at the expression he had put on her face. *Surely I don't look like that! So calculating, so hard.*

She moaned. *He hates me!*

At the sound, Harry whirled around. His eyes widened as he took in the sight of her. "Ah! I thought I heard someone. It is Clarence the page again, I see. That uniform is getting a bit bedraggled, Miss Eardley. Time to spend a bit more from your vast fortune for another one. Or perhaps Winkham will purchase you a whole wardrobe of male clothing after you are wed."

Bella was surprised by the venom in his voice. "They took away my suit when I returned from Somerset House that day."

"I don't suppose it would occur to you to wear a dress. I am beginning to wonder if there is something peculiar about you." Forgetting that he had just cleaned his brush, Curzon dipped it in some ivory paint that was still on his palette, and began over-painting the large canvas in long, angry brush strokes, starting in the lower left-hand corner.

"It is hard to climb down a drainpipe in a dress."

He stopped to turn and glare at her. "Why am I surprised? Your word means nothing, after all."

"There was no other way. They'd locked me in my room."

"I thought you could defeat all locks!"

"And posted a footman outside my door. I had to see you and explain—"

"I am not interested in explanations. I went to Winkham's home and waited for him after the ball. I was sure you were being forced into this match, but that suggestion put him on his high ropes. Said he wouldn't marry an unwilling woman. Said you made no demur at all. Rather, you accepted him with alacrity, and reassured him last night that you were willing."

"Yes, but I can explain—"

"Just answer one question, without roundaboutation: Is this engagement a ruse, or are you really planning to marry him?"

"I . . ."

At her hesitation, Curzon turned back to the painting, which he attacked with renewed vigor. "Go home, Bella. If you can consider marrying the duke, I have nothing to say to you."

"Won't you let me explain why? I walked all the way over from Mayfair to tell you—"

"You should have spared yourself the effort," he growled. "I don't want you here. I have better things to do with my time than listen to your lies. I am trying to clear my things out so I can vacate this studio."

"Vacate?" She looked around, really seeing for the first time the evidence of packing. "Why? Where are you taking your paintings?"

"I expect they'll go into my father's attics. Now please leave!"

Anger began building in Isabella, anger and desperation. *He isn't going to listen to me.* She had to think of a way to buy some time, to get him in a more reasonable frame of mind.

"No! Not until you pay your debts."

"My debts?" He turned back to her. "What the devil?"

"You owe me a nude posing session. You got your kiss, and then some, but you never posed for me."

Fury reddened Curzon's face. "I might have known. That's why you really came here. You risked your life for art, not to square things with me. Art! Damn art!" He threw down his brush and stalked toward her. "Get out before I throw you out."

"You are a fine one to scold me for not keeping my word!"

"Bella!" He put his hand on her arm and tried to turn her toward the door.

"No! I won't go until you pose for me." She resisted him with surprising strength for one so small.

They glared at each other, barely an inch separating their bodies. "What happened to your sketch from the Academy?" he demanded. "That should have provided you with a good male model."

"My father tore it up!" She gave no ground. Hands on hips, she tilted her head back to stare into his eyes.

Fury pinched Curzon's mouth. "So you really want me to pose nude?"

"You can wear a drape to protect your . . . ah, modesty."

"Very well. I can't have you limited to the pudgy Duke of Winkham for your impressions of the masculine anatomy, can I? Once you see him in his undress, perhaps then you will regret rejecting me!" He began undoing his shirt. Before she could quite catch her breath, she was staring at his bare torso.

Bella had to struggle to avoid melting against him at the sight of that muscular chest, liberally covered with curling hair like tiny golden wires. She kept her chin up so as not to follow their tapering trail down into his breeches.

"I'll need a sketch pad."

He turned and rummaged savagely among his stacked belongings. "Here!" He thrust a huge pad at her. "Where do you want me?"

"On the stool where you posed Virginia. No, wait. I want you to stretch out on the couch, the way you were when I first drew you."

"Just exactly that way?" He arched a deliberately provocative brow at her.

Her lips trembled, and warmth spread through her at the memory of Harrison Curzon's body on that morning, but she lifted her chin pugnaciously. "If you can manage it! I'll need an easel."

He stalked to an easel and dragged it in front of the empty fireplace. "Like this?" Is there enough light?"

The sight of his muscles flexing as he lifted and carried the heavy easel did strange things to Bella's breathing. She nodded, not trusting her voice.

"Very well. Turn your back." He fished a vivid turquoise silk scarf out of the pile of clothes he had tossed on the floor earlier.

Bella did as he ordered, then listened with her heart pounding in her ears to the sound of his disrobing and arranging himself on the sofa.

"Ready."

She turned and looked him over slowly. The vision of all that golden male flesh almost undid her. "I . . . need a charcoal," she said, turning away to search for one. *What I re-*

ally need is to compose myself. I'll look the fool if I run out on this now.

"In the box on the floor in front of the picture I was working on." *You vain fool. What do you think you are doing?* Curzon asked himself. *You should have thrown her out and locked the door.*

Feeling calmer and more in control, Bella walked smartly up to the easel, looked Curzon over with a cool professional eye, and started sketching. The room seemed too warm, somehow, so she pulled off the page's jacket. Silence reigned as she roughly sketched in the sofa and began drawing Harry's muscular form. She looked back and forth from him to her drawing, her tongue sticking out of the left side of her mouth. The act of drawing absorbed her attention so much that she forgot her uncomfortable awareness of Curzon as a man.

In the silence of the room, broken only by the scratch of charcoal against paper, Curzon stared up at Isabella, nursing his anger and resentment. How dare she treat him like an object? How dare she come here at all, after engaging herself to Winkham. *Why has she engaged herself to Winkham?*

Time begat calmness, and he began to regret not allowing her to explain. He promised himself that he would listen, after she had finished her drawing. Calmness allowed him to look at Bella without anger, and with the lessening of his anger grew his awareness of her as a woman. *She is so adorable in that silly page outfit, with her tongue sticking out of her mouth. Petite but perfectly formed. I'd like to draw her in the nude. I wonder if she would agree . . .*

But Curzon tried to make his mind veer away from this dangerous topic, for he found himself skipping from thinking of himself drawing her to a picture of himself making love to her, and . . .

"Harry!"

Her indignant voice recalled him from his increasingly lascivious daydream. He looked up to see that her cheeks were uncharacteristically pink.

"What, Bella?"

"You didn't have to take me at my word." She cast a swift glance at the portion of his anatomy that was wrapped by the silk scarf.

"Sorry, Bella. There's something erotic about posing in the nude. Particularly when the artist is a beautifully made little pocket Venus in form-fitting knee breeches."

Bella's mouth fell slightly open. *There is something erotic about drawing such a magnificent man in the nude, too*, she thought. She looked intently into Curzon's eyes, which seemed uncharacteristically dark just now. *You have his attention. Now is your chance to explain*, she told herself. But explanations seemed much less pressing just now.

Suddenly, the room seemed too close. Heat shimmered between them, and she felt herself drawn to him like a magnet to a lodestone. Her charcoal stick dropped from her hand and broke unheeded at her feet as she walked slowly over to him.

"Bella!" His voice was a warning growl. "Get back to your easel and finish your drawing, or I won't answer for the consequences."

"I just . . . I just want to rearrange you a little." *I have to touch him. Just once.* She reached out a tentative hand. "Prop your head up on your arm." She slid her hand along his muscular biceps. "That way I can get a view of this muscle."

His eyes held hers as he adjusted his position. "Like this?"

"Yes." Her voice was barely a whisper. She couldn't pull

away from him, yet pride prevented her from touching him again. *Why doesn't he kiss me?*

"Or perhaps like this?" He sat up and put his hands behind his head, deliberately flexing muscles that rippled beneath his golden skin.

"Oh!" Unable to resist, Bella leaned forward to touch him again and found herself engulfed in his arms. His mouth came down upon hers in a fiery kiss.

Chapter Sixteen

Momentarily stunned by Curzon's abrupt action, Bella lay passively in his arms as he lowered her to the couch. He left her lips to trail kisses to her ear and down her jawline. Her eyes closed, Bella gave herself up to the exquisite sensations he was creating in her.

Curzon leaned over her, one hand on each side of her head. "You are a wicked little temptress. You know that, don't you?"

She opened her eyes. Quite liking this very close view of his finely sculpted features, she smiled slyly. "I certainly hope so." She did what she had been wanting to do since she first saw him peel off his shirt. She touched his chest, luxuriating in the feel of the curling golden hairs that tickled her palm.

He lowered his head to kiss her again, and this time she met him eagerly. Heat seared her. She arched her body against his.

An hour later, or was it only seconds, he pulled away again. "Ah, Bella! You drive me mad. We must quit now, or I am going to make love to you right here."

For answer she pulled his head back down.

With Herculean effort he levered himself away from her. "Wait. I want you to be sure. I think you are a virgin, and I don't want you to do anything you will regret."

"Oh, no, Harry. Love me! Winkham doesn't deserve for me to be a virgin, for though he thinks I want to marry him, he knows I don't love him."

Curzon's nostrils flared. His eyes first widened, then narrowed with fury. "What! Winkham! Don't tell me you still think you are going to marry him!"

"Harry, *please*! We can talk about it later." She tried to draw him closer, but he sat up, hastily rearranging the silk scarf that was his only cover.

"No. By the heavens! I am an idiot." He dropped his head into his hands. "I've fallen in love with the next Lady Oxford, it seems. Like her, you want a fat, complacent husband, a fine title, and an aspiring artist for a lover, just the first of many, of course. For your information, you heartless, selfish jade, I want . . . wanted . . . more from you than just . . ."

Bella sat up and scooted close to him. "You don't understand, Harry. I truly have no choice. Please, let me explain. I am not heartless. My heart belongs to you. I know now that it always will." She put her arms around him comfortingly. At first he stiffened and strained away from her, but then he raised his head slowly and looked into her eyes. Silent tears were sliding down her cheeks. As usual, they were his undoing.

Touching a long index finger to one tear, he lifted it to his lips. "Don't cry, sweetheart." He tucked her in the circle of his arm. "I'll let you explain. I should have done so when you first arrived, but I was just so angry—no, I'll be honest—hurt. I've never felt such pain as when you confirmed your engagement."

She moaned. "Hurt! Oh, Harry." She cupped his jaw in her small hand. "It seems whatever I do, I must hurt someone." She leaned against him and began to sob silently, overpowered by her situation.

He cradled her against him for a while, stroking her tenderly, and wondering at his own feelings as he did so. He still desired her, yet for the first time in his life a woman's feelings and needs were more important to him than his own.

When her shoulders ceased shaking, he gently put her away from him. "Bella, let me get some clothes on and then you must tell me everything."

June Calvin

She nodded, rubbing at her eyes with her fists. He dressed while she watched him without embarrassment, delighting in his masculine beauty, feeling her heart break at the thought that he might not be hers to love forever.

"May Bertram Eardley rot in hell! I'll kill that monster with my bare hands." Curzon stood up from where he had held Isabella against his side while she told him the story of her father's cruelty, and the bargain her grandmother had made to free her mother from it.

Bella did not for a minute doubt that her beloved would do just that, in his present mood. "No! I can't let you. I can't be responsible for my father's death."

"You cannot tell me you love that unfeeling clod!"

Bella shook her head. "Not anymore, though once upon a time, he was a good father to me, before ambition overtook him. Still, he is a human being. And you mustn't have his life on your conscience."

Curzon paced the studio like a caged tiger for a long while as Bella watched him gloomily. At last he returned to her. "Bella, I won't let you do this. You know what you said a few minutes ago about having to hurt someone?"

She nodded her head.

"I am in the same situation. My father doesn't want me to continue with my art, and I am sorry to say he doesn't want me to marry you, either. If I pursue my own life, if I marry the woman I love, I have to hurt my father. If you marry me, you will hurt your mother. But if we give one another and our future up, we hurt each other, and ourselves."

"But Mother—"

"Look at me, Bella." He sat and turned her toward him, one hand on each shoulder. "You are the only woman I have ever loved. I've fought it, God knows, because you are too young, too tiny, too willful. You are mendacious, unconventional, and unpredictable. We are both selfish and obsessed with our art. I am sure we will argue and fight all of our lives. Your father is a cit, a mushroom my father detests. Your grandmother just as rabidly hates me. But I can't care about all of that. I love you. If you marry Winkham, I will be devastated. *I do not know how I will go on.* Do you understand?"

Eyes wide and mournful, Bella nodded slowly. She slid her hands up his chest and around his neck, then pulled herself up to put her lips tenderly against his. "I can't do that to you, Harry. I love you too much," she whispered against his lips.

He kissed her tenderly, deeply, then drew her into his embrace to whisper soothingly into her ear, "Now that is settled. We can put out heads together and see how best to improve your mother's situation."

"I don't see how it is to be done."

"Neither do I at the moment, but—"

A loud, belligerent voice broke into their reverie. Up the stairwell from the bottom floor it could be heard bellowing out, "Where is she! Which studio is Curzon's, you fool! Take me to it at once."

Jean Maillot's equally belligerent voice announced his fury at being insulted and bossed around.

"Oh, no! My father!"

Curzon sprang up. "This way." Grabbing her hand, he dragged her to the door at the far end of the studio, threw a bolt, and thrust her out onto a rickety stairway. She raced down the steps, Curzon on her heels, his heavy tread shaking the steps so that they seemed in danger of collapsing.

The two of them sprinted down the dark, grim alley and onto Conway Street, where they spotted a hackney. Harrison called, "Wait up!" As soon as it had halted, he opened the door and lifted Bella in, gave an address to the driver, and followed her into the seedy carriage.

"Where are we going?"

"Do you trust me, Bella?"

Her bright blue eyes scolded him for even asking.

"We are going to my home. There I am going to put you in my carriage and take you to The Elms. My mother is there. She will shelter you until I can decide how best to deal with your father."

Bella slid into Harry's arms. "I am so worried about my mother."

"I know, love." Curzon stroked her head, his mind racing with plans.

Bella's stomach gave a long, loud grumble. It was such a mundane sound in the circumstances, they both started laughing. "I haven't had anything to eat since the supper dance last night." She giggled, rubbing herself.

"Come to that, neither have I. We can't linger at my house—your father will come there next. I'll have a cold collation packed to eat in the carriage. And we shall have to do something about clothes. I can't take you to my mother, dressed like this."

Bella looked up at him impishly. "Whyever not? I am told I make a very pretty boy. Perhaps she will take me on as her page."

Curzon tweaked her nose. "None of that around my mother, my girl. She is a dear soul, but conventional to the core."

At Harrison's orders, his servants began scurrying around, preparing a hastily assembled cold collation and locating a maid who was not much taller than Bella. "Bring us her best dress, or one of her uniforms, Metcalf. A clean one. Quickly. It is a matter of some urgency. And have the brougham brought around."

"I am sorry, sir," the Curzon butler replied. Your father took it this morning."

"My father is in town?"

"Yes, sir. Something to do with the king's divorce."

"Then order a hackney. I can't drive Bella through the streets of London in my curricle, and she dressed like a maid."

"Of course not, sir." A grin, swiftly suppressed, showed that Metcalf was having great difficulty in maintaining a good butler's imperturbability, for his master's son was holding and occasionally kissing the young girl who was dressed like a boy.

Curzon impatiently paced the blue drawing room while waiting for the food and clothing to be brought. Bella curled up in a ball on a sofa and instantly fell asleep. Blue circles under her eyes attested to her exhaustion. With reluctance he woke her when the uniform was delivered.

"I'll slip out and let you change here. Sending you upstairs will only give the servants spasms."

Isabella yawned and stretched like a sleepy kitten. Unable to resist, Curzon pulled her off the couch and into his arms, and proceeded to kiss her thoroughly.

A choking sound caused them both to break off their kiss. They turned, bodies still pressed together, to confront Sir Randall, whose eyes were nearly bulging out of his head.

"Father!" Curzon stepped away.

Red-faced, Sir Randall stared at them. "I had heard rumors that you had taken on a young boy as a protégé. That was bad enough, but this!"

"It isn't what you think, Father." Harrison took Isabella's hand and led her forward. "This is Isabella Eardley. You must remember her from our ball at The Elms."

Mr. Curzon looked more closely at the young boy. "Thank God! Though it is bad enough for you to have a gently bred female in your arms, at least . . ." The elder Curzon suddenly sat down, as if his legs had given out.

"It is a long story, sir, but I am taking Bella to my

mother. I must ask you to stand by me in this, even though you doubtless won't approve."

"Doubtless!" Sir Randall snapped.

Curzon hastily explained Bella's situation. Sir Randall's reaction was more temperate than Curzon had expected. Relief that it had not been a boy his oldest son was kissing still made him a little giddy. However, he *did* object.

"I cannot like this. Stealing a young girl from her family and hiding her away . . ."

"I will not allow her to be abused, and her father will surely do so if he can get his hands on her. Now, we must leave immediately, for Mr. Eardley will come here after us."

"I'll run upstairs and change, shall I, Harry, while you talk to your father?" Bella took up the uniform.

"No, there isn't time. He could be here any moment. We'll step out into the hall while you change in here." He motioned his father before him.

As soon as the door was shut behind them, Sir Randall turned on his son. "You can't really mean to marry that hoyden, Harry! Dressed as a boy, running from her parents, kissing you like a . . . a . . . I thought her unsuitable merely because of her father, but now! Your career in politics will be over before it begins."

"Then I shall have to turn my attention to learning how to be a gentleman farmer, shan't I, while you man the political barricades." Harrison did not bother to hide his distaste for such a future.

"That is a disrespectful way of speaking to me, Harry."

"I beg your pardon, sir. I am too concerned about Bella to weigh my words carefully." But the younger man did not look contrite.

Sir Randall shook his head. "This Eardley chit is a deplorable influence on you. I am sorry, but I cannot allow you to take so hurly-burly a female to The Elms. Your mother would be plunged into the middle of a scandal she is ill equipped to deal with."

Harry stared unbelievingly at his father. "I never thought you would let me down, Pater."

"In future years you will realize that I had your best interests at heart. Send that misguided child home to her relatives before it is too late."

"He is right, Harry. It will not do to involve your mother in my problems." Both men turned to see Bella not more than three paces from them. She obviously had heard most of this exchange.

"Bella! You haven't changed clothes. We're going to have to leave now, just as you are." He started toward her.

Bella shook her head. "I have another plan. You are going to take me to Winky, and this costume will be exactly what is wanted! But first I have something to say to you, Sir Randall." She faced the elder Curzon squarely.

"You need to know that your demands on your son are not only cruel, but will actually hurt the cause of reform which you espouse."

"You are a bold hussy, to tell me how to conduct my business!"

"Harry will be a terrible politician—"

"If he continues his association with you, we shall never know!"

She put her hands on her hips, unintimidated. "And to bury him in the country, studying sheep and corn and reading account books is the height of stupidity."

Harrison groaned. "Come on, Bella, pulling caps with my father isn't accomplishing anything." He attempted to take her elbow, but she jerked away.

"No. I haven't done. Sir Randall, have you ever seen any of your son's paintings?"

"Of course I have, you cheeky baggage. They are all over The Elms, and—"

"But have you really looked at them? If you had, you would know that by his artistry, Harry is able to portray the needs of the lower orders, the injustices done to them, in such a way as to plead their cause more effectively than the most inspired oratory. Farm workers, upstairs maids, flower girls—who can look at one of his magnificent studies and fail to know that these are real human beings, worthy of consideration and protection? Until I saw his painting of the one-legged soldier, begging in his tattered uniform, I had never given a thought to the shabby way our veterans have been treated since the war.

"On display in the Royal Academy or in the great houses of England, those paintings can do more to aid the cause of reform than Harry could do in a lifetime of voting in the House of Commons."

Sir Randall opened his mouth and then closed it. His eyes shifted to his son, who was looking at Bella like a man who had been given a great gift, and he had, the elder Curzon realized. His son had been given the pride of knowing his work had real significance instead of being just a rich young man's foolish pastime.

"Furthermore, he loves me. If we are parted, I do not believe he will ever fulfill any of your ambitions or his. A man like Harrison Curzon feels deeply. Yet he loves you, so if he defies you, it will tear him apart. You are exactly like my father!"

"I beg your pardon." Sir Randall indignantly protested. "There is no comparison between myself and that . . . that mushroom!"

"Oh, yes there is. Like my father, you would cripple your child's life to fulfill your own ambitions. Hardly the act of a loving parent!"

A loud, impatient banging of the knocker on the front door cut off Sir Randall's response.

"That is my father." Bella's eyes widened in panic as the footman moved to open the door.

"This way." Curzon tugged on her arm. She turned and ran with him down the tiled entryway toward the door that led to the servants' offices.

"A moment, Harrison. Johnson, don't admit him yet." Sir Randall followed his son, who stopped in the act of opening the door for Bella.

"Did you say you are going to Winkham?"

Harrison looked at Bella questioningly. She nodded, chin up in a stubborn line.

"Harrison, you know there will be unavoidable scandal?"

"Yes, Father. I am sorry for the pain it may bring you and Mother, but I will not abandon Bella. If necessary, I will challenge both Winkham and Eardley."

Sir Randall met his son's icy blue eyes, and the expression he saw there, of determination and pain, made him catch his breath. Bella's words were confirmed in that finely drawn countenance. *Duel or no duel, he is lost to me if I continue to oppose him.*

"I hope you are worthy of my son's love," he said sternly to Bella.

"I love him with all my heart, too much to permit him to fight a duel for me, particularly as I have heard that he is not a good shot, and both my father and Winkham are expert marksmen. At the very least, my plan will free me from my engagement to Winkham. It might possibly free my mother and gain Father's approval as well."

Sir Randall lifted quizzical eyebrows. "Are you a magician, then?"

Harrison grinned. "She is very resourceful, sir. Whatever her scheme is, I'd not wager against it."

The doors shook with Bertram Eardley's pounding, and his loud voice could be heard demanding entrance.

Sir Randall drew a deep breath. "Take the brougham,

then; you won't want to drive her through the streets like that. I'll have it sent round to the mews. I'll keep Eardley tied up for a while." He held out his hand to his son, who grasped his wrist in a firm clasp. Throat working, Harrison could only nod. Then he broke away and thrust Bella past the door.

Sir Randall turned back to where his servants awaited his orders. "Johnson, when I have had a moment to settle myself in the drawing room, open the door and announce my visitor to me in the usual way."

Johnson, like the butler, had been an interested observer of the confrontation with Isabella. "And if he is calling for Mr. Harrison, sir?"

"Say nothing. Show him to me anyway."

Chapter Seventeen

Harrison took the basket of food from his cook just as the surprised servant was tucking a bottle of wine under the napkin. Swinging it up without missing a stride, he continued out the kitchen door and down the alley toward the mews, Bella taking two steps to his one to keep up with him.

True to his word, Sir Randall sent the brougham around; it arrived within minutes of Harrison's ordering another team harnessed.

"We won't need fresh horses," Bella objected.

"I don't know what you have in mind, but if it doesn't work, we might." Harrison's mouth firmed. He urged her into the carriage while he supervised the change. By the time he joined her, five minutes later, she had already delved into the basket and was chewing ecstatically on a sandwich with thin slices of ham protruding from the bread.

Enchanted as ever by her natural, zestful behavior, Curzon laughed out loud. "Did you save me anything?" He helped himself to a meat pie. "I've told the coachman to drive around for a few minutes while we batten ourselves."

"Mmmpf," Bella managed, nodding approvingly.

After fifteen minutes of intense concentration on her food and wine, Bella sighed contentedly. "Much better."

"Now you can tell me what your plan is." Harrison licked some crumbs from one aristocratic finger, then leaned forward to remove a crumb clinging to the side of Bella's mouth the same way.

"If you do that again, I will forget my plan entirely," she sighed, closing her eyes and holding her mouth up for a kiss.

When he had obliged her, Harrison pulled away. "Now—let us have your plan without further delay."

"Very well." She sat up straight. "Winkham wants to marry me because I am short and pretty. He thinks I have good manners and knows that I am generally accepted by the *ton*."

"And because I want you. He was disgustingly gleeful at having triumphed over me."

"Well, I will give him a disgust of me. One look at me in these breeches should do it, especially with you as my escort!"

Harrison nodded. "Without a doubt, but it seems pointless. Winkham's withdrawal from your engagement is not the main obstacle, after all. If it had been, you would have done it without all of this commotion, I am sure. Let us just be off for Scotland. Every minutes counts, for I make no doubt your father will pursue us."

"You haven't heard all of it. I am going to beg him *not* to cry off."

Harrison scowled at her. "What May Game is this?"

"It was always my intention to give him a disgust of me, but I planned to wait until the end of the season, perhaps even after my father had departed for the country. That way Father couldn't immediately wed me to another of his cronies. But when I learned of the bargain my grandmother had struck with him—"

"Bella, we've been over this."

"Don't you see? He'll be very easy to discourage. I'll stand before Winky dressed like this, allude to having been with you at your studio, and ask him to allay my father's wrath. When he understands just how improper my behavior has been, he will want no more of me, but I will beg him not to break our engagement. He'll insist that I do it, if I make myself sufficiently obnoxious to him. I'll refuse. Then we'll go home. He will follow me there, and I will give my father a chance for a strategic retreat in front of him."

"I don't—"

"Faced with having Winkham know I'd been forced into accepting his suit, or having him think I'd done so willingly as part of a scheme to get my parents back together—"

"I don't quite follow . . ."

"It may not work. But my father desperately wants Winkham's good opinion. He would not want him to know how brutal he has been to me and my mother. I'm hoping to maneuver him into appearing to be insisting on a separation from my mother, which I, loving daughter that I am, have been trying to prevent by marrying the man of his choosing."

Harrison sat back against the squabs, frowning. "That is a subtle scheme. I hadn't had the opinion that your father was a subtle person."

Bella snorted. "No, indeed! I will have to explain it to him. Oh, I don't know. It may all be a disaster, but at least I must try. For my mother's sake, I *must!*

"I know you must. Gallant little lady. But this scheme doesn't seem likely to further *my* cause with your father."

She sighed. "It is just barely possible that he will fear that I've been so compromised that we must marry."

"I hate to have anyone think that of you."

"Or of you."

Harrison's lips twitched. "I am sure many members of the *ton* will not be in the least surprised to hear it of me, your formidable grandmother among them. Well, then, we shall try it. If it does not work . . ."

"There is always Gretna Green. Harry, you must promise me that no matter what happens you won't allow yourself to be forced into a duel."

He shook his head slowly. "I am sorry, Bella, that I cannot do. A man's honor places certain requirements upon him."

Bella wrapped her arms around herself and shuddered. "Then it has to work. It just has to!"

The tall clock in the duke's hall was chiming noon when Bella and Harrison were admitted to Winkham's upstairs sitting room. He emerged fifteen minutes later, yawning and showing every signs of a hasty toilette. He had even forgotten to don a neckcloth.

The dev . . . dickens! What on earth!" Winkham stopped stock-still to stare at Bella, who stood when he entered. His eyes swept up and down her trim form, well revealed in the tight breeches.

"I wanted you to hear about it from my own lips, Winky. You mustn't blame Harrison, for it was all my doing, and he brought me here straightaway!"

Winkham visibly recoiled from the sight of his betrothed wearing male clothing. "What can you be about, appearing in such attire! Hope no one has seen you."

"Oh, no one saw me, for we came in a closed carriage." She let that scandalous tidbit sink in for a few seconds, and then continued, "No one who knows me, anyway. Except servants, of course, but they don't matter. Oh, and the porter at Harry's studio, and perhaps Mr. Maillot . . ."

"Harry's studio?"

"Yes. I went there when I couldn't get a hackney to take me home."

"But what . . . ? Why . . . ?"

"My father locked me in my room, and I couldn't climb down the drainpipes in a skirt, you see."

"Drainpipes . . ." The duke was clearly reeling.

"You are making micefeet of this explanation, Bella," Curzon admonished her.

"You see, Winky, I like to walk around the city in men's clothing. It is so confining being a female. Dressed like this I can go anywhere I want. But I walked too far, and was too tired, and had no money to get a hackney, so I went to Harrison's studio to rest and catch a ride home."

"Good Gawd, Harrison. Should have taken her straight home, got some decent clothes on her."

"My father showed up before he could do so. I could hear him at the bottom of the stairs. He would think the worst, of course, when he found me alone with Harry, which is why I ran down the back stairway. You must speak to him, explain for me."

"Wait a minute. How long were you with Harry in his studio?" Winkham turned toward the tall blond man who sat listening to Bella, a frown wrinkling his forehead. "I didn't know you *had* a studio, Harry. Come to that, how did *you* know, Bella?"

"Why, I've gone there often. It's in Fitzroy Square. A fascinating area, not at all like Mayfair. And Harrison has been good enough to teach me—"

"Have you gone there alone often?" Winkham's manner grew even stiffer.

"No, of course not. Except for today, that is. And—oh, yes, another time when it was raining. Harry was asleep that time, so I warmed up by his fire while I sketched him until he woke up and kissed me—oh, if you are going to look so beastly, I am going to leave. Come along, Harrison. He is not going to be any help." She stood and raced from the room.

"Harry, I think you owe me an explanation."

"I'm not sure I can add anything to what she has said. A rare treat of a female you've gotten yourself engaged to, Winkham. I'd better follow her, get her home, or there's no telling what else she'll get up to. If I were you, I'd ask her to end the engagement."

"I heard that, Harrison Curzon!" Bella stuck her nose back in the door. "Some help *you* are!" Winky mustn't cry off, he mustn't! I won't let him!"

"You told me she truly wanted to marry you, but I doubted you." Curzon shook his head wonderingly.

"Not quite as pleased with that thought this morning," Winkham growled. "If this is some sort of scheme to make me cry off, it is very near to working."

"It is not! You mustn't cry off. That would ruin my plans. And don't forget that kiss at Vauxhall!" She shook her finger at him. "Society will judge very ill of you for compromising me that way and then not marrying me. Now, you know you like my father, Winky, and you are like a son to him, the son he never had. You'd break his heart if you cried off."

"I like Bertram very well, but I never signed on for a wife who parades herself in men's clothing and calls on other men in their studios. Been leery of your feelings for Harry all along, but you accepted my proposal so promptly . . ."

"Not other men, just Harry. I love Harry, you see. But you knew I didn't love you, didn't you?"

"Thought you were fond of me . . ."

"And so I am," she cooed. Curzon's eyebrows shot up at this declaration.

"Thought you wanted to marry me!"

"And so I do. That is . . ." Bella dropped her eyes and dug her toes into the carpet. "I want to marry the man my father picked for me, you see . . ."

Winkham's eyes goggled. "Hadn't marked you for such a dutiful daughter!"

"Oh, if you are going to be like that!" Bella once more stalked out of the room.

"Come back here, Bella. You can't go out on the streets of London dressed like that. Not while you're still engaged to me. I'll take you to your father."

Bella eased back into the room, a winning smile on her face. "Would you, Winky? I knew you would! What an understanding husband you are going to be. See, I told you, Harry. Winky won't be one of those tiring old domestic tyrants." She grabbed Harrison's arm and gave it an intimate squeeze.

Winkham roared, "I damn sure am not going to be an understanding husband. If you love Curzon, get *him* to marry you! You march yourself right home and tell your father you are crying off!"

I would be very happy to marry Isabella," Curzon said, "but she has some mysterious reason why she cannot."

"That don't signify to me."

"Well, I *won't* cry off, so there. If you want our engagement to end, you shall have to be the one to cry off. Otherwise . . ." Isabella wrung her hands and screwed up her face as if she were going to cry. "Otherwise something dreadful will happen. Though I expect it will, either way. Oh, Winky! You will still stand my father's friend, won't you?"

"Not if he's forced you into this engagement after promising me there was no one else, that your only reluctance was about marrying at all. 'Silly notion of a career as a painter,' he said. 'Has to marry someone,' he said, 'might as well be you. She's fond of you,' he said. Ha! Never told me you were in love with someone else, or touched in the upper works, for that matter, as you surely must be to wear such . . . vulgar attire!"

Bella raced over to Winkham and caught hold of his arm, looking up into his face imploringly. "No, you mustn't blame Father. I meant to marry to please him. He didn't know any different."

Winkham groaned. "This is all very perplexing."

"You're like a son to him, Winky. He will be cut up terribly if you drop him. If I am to cry off, you must go to him and tell him that you will continue the friendship. If you won't, I won't cry off. You'll have to marry me or face the censure of the entire *ton*."

"Curzon, don't you have something to say to this? You won't let her marry someone else if you love her, surely."

Harrison shook his head slowly. "I can't force her to marry me. I can't imagine anything more fraught with the possibility for disaster than marrying Bella if she doesn't wish it. She'll be a difficult enough wife, as it is."

Winkham winced at the irrefutable truth of this observation. "Give me a moment," he snapped. He turned back into his bedroom and emerged minutes later with his neckcloth hastily tied.

"Let's go. Harry, you won't want to be with us, I am sure."

"Oh, I think I shall. Mr. Eardley will doubtless be entertaining certain notions about me. I intend to be there to defend myself. Our carriage is out front."

While Bella and Harrison confronted the Duke of Winkham, Bertram Eardley was confronting Sir Randall. He stomped into the drawing room right behind Metcalf, elbowing him out of the way to demand, "Where's my daughter! That rake of a son of yours has abducted my daughter!"

Sir Randall was surprised to find the Dowager Duchess of Carminster trailing her son-in-law into the room. He stood on seeing her, and gave her a polite bow.

"Duchess. Mr. Eardley. Be seated, if you please. We have much to discuss."

"Then you know about it! There'll be no discussion. I'll call that insolent puppy out! Tell me where Bella is, instantly."

"Sit down, Bertram." The duchess gave him her most quelling look as she took a seat. "Let us hear what Sir Randall has to say."

"Don't matter a flit what he has to say," Eardley grumbled, though he did as the duchess commanded. "Ain't"

going to let my Bella throw herself away on Harrison Curzon, damn his hide—no title, shocking reputation, whole
family has ice water in its veins—no!"

"If you are saying that my family is not good enough to
unite with yours, I think *I* may have to call *you* out," Sir
Randall snarled.

"Gentlemen, this is getting us nowhere. Sir Randall, I
take it that Bella is indeed with Harrison, and that they plan
to marry. Are they eloping, then?"

"I don't believe so. In fact, if you will return home and
await events, Mr. Eardley, I think they will come to you
there."

"Await events? Await events? My daughter jauntering
about town unchaperoned with that . . . that rake, and you
want me to await events. He's likely halfway to Gretna
now. Abducting heiresses would be just in his line."

"Such a touching show of paternal affection, though I received the impression from Miss Eardley that you were not
exactly a tender parent."

Eardley's face turned a dangerous shade of red. "My relationship with my daughter is of no concern to you."

"No, nor your relationship with your wife. Unless, of
course, your behavior affects my son adversely. Come, let
us be plain. Neither of us seeks an alliance with the other,
but our children have established a bond of affection
and—"

"Damn your affection. She is going to marry the Duke of
Winkham, and that's the end of it."

Turning away from Eardley as from a lost cause, Sir
Randall addressed the duchess. "I am surprised to see you
lending yourself to this determined thwarting of your
granddaughter's affections."

Two spots of color appeared high on the duchess's pale
cheeks. She drew herself up proudly. "As Bertram said, this
is a family matter."

"Hmmmm. Very well, then, I shall say no more. I am late to attend the king, at any rate. The divorce proceedings, you know. I see that Carminster is in town."

"The king gave him little choice in the matter, or I assure you he would not be." The duchess had no wish to discuss the son who had distanced himself from his family upon his disastrous marriage. She sought to change the subject. "I would not have thought you would wish to attend the trial. I have heard that it is insufferably hot and uncomfortable in the House of Lords, not to speak of a very irritating proceeding."

"Too true. However, like Carminster, I have been given no choice in the matter. Having newly succeeded to the title of the Earl of Bramtham, I am expected to attend."

Bertram Eardley gave a little start at this. "You, the Earl of Bramtham? Thought that title was extinct."

"In abeyance. The last of the line was a female. But as our family is a distant connection, and the king has been casting around for a title for me, matters were set in train for me to inherit. She passed to her eternal reward but a fortnight ago. I learned of it yesterday at the same time that the king commanded me to attend the trial."

"Humph. Didn't know you were a king's man." Eardley's voice revealed a grudging approval.

"Royal favor can often be gained by generosity to the royal purse. Since you are so impressed by titles, you might take that notion under advisement."

The duchess's brow wrinkled in puzzlement. "I am surprised the king was so eager to have you join the Lords now, though. Surely he knows you have been on friendly terms with his wife."

"So I have been. But her behavior in Italy deserves close scrutiny. I mean to hear the evidence without prejudice."

Eardley stood abruptly. "This ain't getting my Bella back. Come, Your Grace."

The duchess used her cane to rise. "I bid you good day, Sir . . . ah, that is, Lord Bramtham."

He moved to take her hand. "You are among the first to call me that. How strange it sounds. My wife will doubtless find it startling to be called countess!" He cast a significant look at Eardley as he said this.

"Hmmmm!" Seeing the bait, Eardley resisted the urge to rise to the lure. But he made a respectful bow to his host before offering the duchess his arm and escorting her from the room.

Lord Bramtham sank back into his chair as they left. He felt a guarded optimism. Eardley had continued to pose and bluster, but clearly the news that Harrison Curzon was in line for a title had made a favorable impression. *I little dreamt when I sought a title, Harry, that I would be hoping it would secure to you a little hoyden for a bride!*

In the carriage Bertram Eardley fumed and fidgeted. "Thinks I'll let his son marry my daughter, settle for being a countess, when she can be a duchess. Hah! He despises me. Wouldn't do a thing for me in society, no more than did your family. Why should I ally myself to him? Winkham and I get along famously, like father and son. What do you say to that!"

"I say that you have paid an enormous price in your quest for a title for your daughter." The duchess turned her head away from him, presenting a stony profile.

"Price! Price! Ain't had to pay Winkham a penny. There's Bella's fortune from her grandfather, o'course, but it wasn't an object with him."

The duchess said nothing.

"Come on, you old besom. What do you mean?"

She turned slightly, looking down at him. "I mean you have alienated your daughter utterly. When she first came to me, she was merely exasperated with you, but now she despises you as much as your wife does. But I doubt a woman's feelings matter a whit to you."

"A dutiful wife and daughter would be guided by me, and not by their errant emotions!" Eardley thrust out his chin aggressively. "And mind you, if Winkham slips his lead, that's just what will happen. I'll find a husband to my liking for Bella, and take Seraphina back to Hertfordshire with me, just you wait and see if I don't."

The duchess clutched her cane until her knuckles turned white, resisting the strong urge to rap her son-in-law across his head with it. "You bellowed out her name and threats of retribution against Curzon for ruining her all over the city of London. After this day's work, you may find yourself exceedingly grateful if you can manage to marry her to a coal merchant!"

Chapter Eighteen

Bella nestled in the curve of Harrison's arm on the short drive from the Duke of Winkham's to Carminster House. She chewed on her lower lip, ignoring the fulminating glances the duke gave her. When the carriage stopped, she moved forward, ready to jump from it immediately.

The duke put out a restraining hand to catch her arm. "Wait, Isabella! That's Lady Jersey and Mrs. Drummond Burrell walking along the street." His voice reflected his awe of two of the *ton*'s most influential females. "You don't want them to see you dressed like that."

Bella turned her head, her eyes seeking Curzon's. Her brows were lifted as if awaiting the answer to a question, and a mischievous twinkle lit her eyes. He grinned at her and nodded, whereupon she pushed down the latch and sprang from the carriage before the footman could even set down the steps for her. She landed hard on both feet directly in front of two of society's most proper ladies.

"Oh! I do beg your pardon. I didn't mean to startle you, Lady Jersey, Mrs. Burrell." She essayed a curtsey, gripping an imaginary skirt in her hands.

The horrified matrons stared at the apparition in front of them, a disheveled young girl dressed like a page, her form-fitting knee breeches considerably the worse for wear.

"Isabella Eardley? Is that you?" squawked Mrs. Burrell.

"Yes, ma'am. I expect you are wondering why I am dressed like this. I can explain—"

"Perhaps you'd better not." The duke emerged from the carriage to take her elbow.

Curzon followed Winkham out of the carriage. "He's right, Bella. Take too long. Your father has first claim upon your time."

Lady Jersey turned to the woman at her side. "And riding in a closed carriage with two young men."

"One of them a notorious rake!" Mrs. Burrell joined her companion in tilting up her nose and walking away without bidding any of the three a polite farewell.

Bella looked over her shoulder at Curzon, laughter dancing in her eyes. "You should have let me explain, Winky. There is no telling what they will spread around."

Moaning slightly, the duke marched her up the steps past the astonished footman who was opening the door. Just inside it the usually imperturbable butler's eyes bulged as he saw her in her page's uniform.

"Miss Bella!"

"Where is my father, Hilliard?"

"In the Egyptian salon with Her Grace and your mother, miss."

"No need to announce us." Bella led the two men quickly to the drawing room and pushed open the door without scratching.

Her mother's face was buried in a large white kerchief, while her husband stood over her, berating her. The sound of her sobs tore at Bella's heart.

The duchess was standing by the window. She had obviously seen their arrival, for she was facing the door, waiting for them with a very peculiar expression on her face.

Bella's heart pounded and her stomach clenched. *I must succeed. So much is at stake!* "Hello, Father, Mother, Grandmother. Look who I have brought with me."

"Bella! Isabella Eardley!" Her father bit off his scold at her mother to storm over to her. "Where have you been? What in the name of all that is holy are you wearing? Get upstairs and change clothes immediately."

Then he saw the duke hesitantly following Isabella. Behind him stood Harrison Curzon. "She . . . she was with you, Winkham?" he asked hopefully.

"She came to my home a short while ago to ask me not to cry off. Dressed as she is, and in the company of Harrison Curzon, you can imagine how well that request sat with me."

All of Bertram Eardley's hopes were crashing to dust. Seeing the disgust in the duke's face, he guessed that all hope of hunting with the Quorn was gone. Without caring who was there, Bertram raised his fist to his daughter. "You little bitch!"

"Wait, Father. You must hear what I have to say! Please, you'll regret it to your dying day if you don't." Bella stood up to the raised fist without flinching, though Harrison had thrust the duke aside, ready to protect her.

"You'd best do as she says." The duchess was at Eardley's elbow. "Sit down and calm yourself, Bertram. This is a situation that calls for a cool head."

"Yes, do sit down, Bertie. No need for violence, I trust." The duke eyed Bella's father uneasily.

Eardley's face reddened. He seemed to swell with fury as he turned on Curzon. "Harrison Curzon, you'll answer to me for this outrage!"

Bella's heart pounded with terror that her father was going to challenge her beloved to a duel. "*Please* listen to Winky, Father."

"Sit *down*, Bertram!" The duchess's commanding voice cut across Bella's plea. Eardley clenched and unclenched his fist, but finally heeded Winkham and the duchess. He trod heavily to a chair and flung himself down. The duchess also sat, her body held rigidly at the edge of her seat, both hands on the cane in front of her.

Breathing out a sigh of relief, Bella politely invited the duke and Curzon to sit also, before going to place a comforting hand on her mother's shoulder.

"Father, I want you to know that I did what I did to try to save your marriage."

Whatever he had been expecting to hear, this was not it. Eardley could only gape at his daughter. Instead of looking at him, though, she directed her remarks to the duke.

"When I told you I would marry you, I meant it, Your Grace. But I knew then, though I had never told anyone, that my heart belonged to Harrison."

A slight intake of breath told her that the duchess was as surprised by this less than accurate confession as her father, who remained uncharacteristically speechless. Her mother lowered her handkerchief and looked up uncertainly at her daughter.

"You see, Winky, my father and mother have been unhappy together for quite some time—"

"Now see here," Eardley found his voice to protest.

"Don't interrupt, Father. As matters stand now, His Grace is under the *mistaken* notion that you were forcing me to wed him. That thought naturally made him angry, for he is too proud and kind a man to wish a bride who doesn't want to marry him, who is in fact in love with another."

"And been in some dam . . . dashed compromising positions with him, too," the duke muttered.

"If he continues to believe that, he will not want to have *anything further to do with you.*" Bella's emphatic pronunciation of this sentence caused Eardley to shudder. His jaw tightened ominously.

Bella rushed on. "But once he realizes that it is I, not you, who have deceived him, I am sure he will still value you as he ought."

Bertram Eardley opened his mouth, gaped like a dying fish for a moment or two, and then shut it.

"I knew that you felt my mother's family had in some measure cheated you by snubbing you for so many years. I thought if I made it up to you by marrying a duke, one who obviously liked and respected you, you might forgive Mother and not insist on the separation that you have had the lawyers draw up."

The duchess let out another soft gasp. Bella felt her mother's shoulder quiver nervously beneath her hand.

"But I hadn't reckoned with how much I love Harry, or how much that would upset Winky. I hope you can all forgive me for the deception."

Bertram Eardley was not a subtle man, but he was not a stupid one, either. Every person in the room was looking at him expectantly, and the Duke of Winkham's gaze had a hard edge to it. Eardley could see this cherished friendship slipping from his grasp.

Slowly, feeling his way, he responded, "Bella, you should have discussed all of this with me. I take it you *want* her to cry off, Winkham?"

The duke nodded. "Even if she didn't love Curzon, not the wife for me. Look at the way she is dressed. I think she is touched in the upper works. Lady Jersey and Mrs. Drummond Burrell saw her as we arrived. It'll be all over London by nightfall. I've no wish for a notorious bride."

Bella jumped in saying, "But even if I do cry off, you'll still want Father to come hunting with you, won't you, Winky?"

The duke clearly understood Bella's subtle blackmail, for he responded just as she hoped he would. "Of course. Looking forward to it. Know you're a bruising rider. And still want to breed my sow to Monarch, your champion hog. Start a new line, won't we, Bertie?"

Eardley nodded his head eagerly. "That we will, m'boy. That we will. England has never seen such hams as they'll produce."

The duchess leaned forward on her cane. "Now, Bella, you mustn't be upset by the separation. It is what both Bertram and Seraphina want, after all. I'm sure the duke will agree that a clean and complete break is best. Your father has already agreed that your mother may make her home with me. Having done that, he won't want to continue to be financially responsible for her, will you, Bertram?"

Eardley glared at her, but nodded his head. "Can't let a female out from under my nose with the right to run up debts against me. No, indeed. We'll do it up all legal."

Bella tried her best to look disappointed, but the corner of her mouth was quivering. "I'm truly sorry for having interfered."

Seraphina raised a trembling hand to grasp hers and squeezed it hard. "You are a good daughter, Bella. I know you thought you were acting for the best."

"Then the engagement to the Duke of Winkham has been terminated?" Curzon's anxious look was in sharp contrast to the ill-concealed joy on his beloved's face. "Dare I hope, sir, that you will be willing to hear a proposal from me?"

Eardley's mouth turned down, and his face began to redden. "By no means, I—"

"Of course you will, Bertram." The duchess thumped her cane on the floor for emphasis. "The girl's been ruined. You bellowed her name and Curzon's all over London, the duke's servants saw her arrive unchaperoned with a notorious rake, and she has appeared before Lady Jersey and Mrs. Burrell dressed like a boy, after having just exited a closed carriage with not one but two gentlemen. Remember what I said in the carriage about her marriage prospects? They are even slimmer now."

Eardley snarled. "I can find a husband for her. An heiress, after all!"

"Marriage to the son of the Earl of Bramtham is not a bad match. The boy is rich, too, or at least his father is. Doubt he'd make any demands on your purse."

Breathing a silent thank you to his father for obtaining

the title, Curzon quickly seconded the duchess's suggestion. "All I want is Bella, sir."

Eardley's mouth worked, but no sound came out. Clearly, he hated to let Isabella and Curzon win.

"The Earl of Bramtham? When did this happen?" the duke asked Harrison.

"News to me, Winky. Knew there was a possibility, but hadn't any idea when or if it would actually materialize. There you are, Bella. You'll be a countess someday." Curzon did not look at Bella to see what effect this announcement had. His eyes were on Bertram Eardley, who looked as if he had just bitten into a rotten oyster.

The duke leaned forward. "If you want my opinion, Bertie . . . ?"

Eardley hesitated a moment and then nodded.

"Think you'd better give her to him. Not many men'd want her if they knew what an unconventional creature she is. Did you know she has made it a practice to walk around London by herself, dressed as a man? That she has visited Harry's studio alone several times? No other man will want her if it gets out, and it will. Things do. If you asked me, Curzon's dicked in the nob to want her, but since he does . . ."

Eardley gripped the arms of his chair until his knuckles were white. "Bella, I ought to . . ."

Winkham continued in a firm voice, "I'd like the termination of our engagement to be announced right away. I don't want anything to distract attention from the bill I am going to introduce in the fall session concerning the government grants to build modern swine sheds. If you are going to continue helping me round up votes, you can't afford public scandal. Your best hope of minimizing gossip will be to see her wed quickly—Harry can get a special license—and then they had best leave London, perhaps even leave England for a year or two, till the talk dies down. Bella, you were always prattling about touring the great houses and museums of Italy. Perhaps Harry could take you there for a long honeymoon trip."

Bella bounded away from her stand by her mother's chair and across the room to throw her arms around the duke. "Winky, I love you. You are going to be my brother, the brother I never had! That is just the thing, don't you think, Harry?"

Harry was watching Eardley closely, and saw the moment when resignation tamped down the red in his face. "Yes, Bella, I do, but you are kissing the wrong man." He held out his arms, and she bounced over to him, throwing herself on his lap and kissing him joyfully on the lips without any regard for the remonstrations of her grandmother. Then all eyes in the room turned to look questioningly at Eardley.

"Damn all, I expect that is what has to be done. Very well, Curzon. Go see the archbishop. We'll do it tomorrow morning if you can get the license today. And Bella, go upstairs and change clothes. You look like a cheap tart of an actress dressed for a breeches part."

"Yes, Father," Bella responded demurely.

The duke stood, relief on his face. "That's it, then! Well, I must be off. I'm late for the trial. Wretched thing is like to keep me pinned in London for weeks! Shall I have my Buttercup sent on to your boar when the time comes?"

Eardley stood, too, and clapped the duke on the shoulder. "Tell you what. If you're still tied up, I'll journey up there meself, escort her down. Wouldn't want to trust her to servants."

"Excellent." The duke and Eardley strolled companionably from the room, discussing the best way to transport a prize sow.

The duchess sank back against her chair, her skin the color of paper. Her breath escaped her in a long, soft hiss. Suddenly, she looked every one of her eighty-one years.

"Grandmother!"

"Mother!"

The two younger women ran to succor her, patting her cheeks and feeling her forehead.

"Shall I send for the doctor?" Harrison asked, hovering behind them.

"My vinaigrette! It's in my reticule," Seraphina shrieked, pointing him to the small purse that had fallen beside her chair.

A low moan escaped the duchess.

"Oh, Grandmama! I'll never forgive myself if I've made you ill." Bella dared to stroke the proud gray head.

The duchess struggled to sit up, and when she had succeeded, waved away the vinaigrette. "I'll be all right directly. I have never been so terrified in my life. Such a near-run thing. Isabella, what an ingenious . . . You've saved Seraphina and yourself, too."

Her color rose as the duchess absorbed the full impact of the last few minutes. "My dear child!" She suddenly embraced her granddaughter enthusiastically. Tears of joy coursing down her cheeks, she turned to Harry. "You'd better do as he says, and get that license before he has a chance to change his mind."

"I'm on my way." Harrison grinned, tipped his hat to the two ladies, and left the room.

After he had closed the door behind him, Isabella's mother spoke up, hesitant but worried. "Oh, Bella, I don't know about that man. Everyone says he's a rake."

"And so I expect he is, Mama. But he's my rake, and I'm going to see that his rakish days are over!"

Chapter Nineteen

Harrison Curzon was terrified. It was his wedding night, and his mouth was dry, his hands clammy. He paced his bedroom floor nervously. *Bella will be wondering. I've got to go in there.*

He looked up at the ceiling as if for inspiration, but its painting of rosy maidens and leering satyrs only underscored the source of his anxiety.

What do I know about initiating a virgin into the art of lovemaking? he thought despairingly. *I've precious little experience of making love with ladies, and certainly none with innocents.* Memories of the disgust and rejection with which Davida Gresham and Virginia Douglas had received his kisses seared him. Desperately, he reminded himself that Bella had welcomed his kisses from the first and seemed eager to consummate their marriage.

But that is because she is an innocent. She doesn't know what it entails. And she is so small. What if I hurt her? Curzon groaned at the thought of the way he seemed to lose control when kissing Bella.

He stopped at the window and leaned forward, both hands on the sash, gloomily studying the wet London streets as if they held some answer.

"Harry?"

He whirled around. Bella stood looking uncertainly up at him. She was barefooted. Her freshly washed hair coiled in tight ringlets around her flushed face. Wearing an ordinary white nightrail, she looked ridiculously young and virginal, wholly adorable, and utterly terrifying.

"Bella, you shouldn't be here! I . . ."

"What's wrong, Harry? Why haven't you come to me?"

Bella tilted her head back, sorrow in her heart as she looked up at her husband. He looked even more handsome than usual in a wine red brocade dressing gown, his blond curls in disarray, one lock dangling on his forehead in a manner that made her palms itch with the desire to smooth it back into place. But he also had a grim expression on his face that doubled her anxiety. Why hadn't he come to her room by now? She had spent the hours since their sudden betrothal yearning for the moment when they could be alone together, and yet she had been forced to come to his room and accost him.

He looks angry! Pain ripped through Bella. *Does he feel that he was forced into marrying me?*

It was hard to believe. He had lost no time in obtaining the special license. By the time the duchess's lawyer had been summoned to put the finishing touches on the separation agreement between her mother and father, he had already obtained a special license and was back at Carminster House, planning where they were to go for the first night of their marriage. Then he had seemed happy, full of plans for their future. *But now!* Bella bit the corner of her lower lip nervously. *Now he looks like he wishes I would disappear.*

"Do you regret marrying me? I know it all happened so quickly, but . . ."

He moved away from the window. "I don't regret marrying you, Bella. I'm just . . ." He chuckled ruefully, running his fingers through his hair. "I guess you could say I've got a case of wedding nerves."

"You? I don't understand. You've had so many women, Harry."

He flinched. "Don't remind me! That is part of the problem." He tugged at his earlobe, a pained expression distorting his features.

Bella felt a sick dread seizing her. This was her deepest fear, that the very experienced Harrison Curzon would find her a boring and inept lover. As the moments had ticked by while she waited for him to join her in their marriage bed, her fears had grown. *How can I hope to please a man who has known some of London's most beautiful and sophisticated women?*

She shivered with apprehension. "Oh, Harry, I'm afraid . . . I won't . . . can't . . ." Tears of despair slid from her eyes. "Perhaps we should just talk. We could sit here and discuss . . . oh, perspective, or something." She took his hand and tugged him toward the small sofa in front of the fireplace. He sat gingerly beside her, as far from touching her as the small sofa would allow.

He continued to stare at her as if she were an unwanted visitor he was trying to figure out how to encourage to leave. Desperately, she cast about for a topic of conversation.

"I thought it was brilliant of you to invite Winky to be your groomsman, and then suggest that while he was there he could witness the separation agreement. Father had us all terrified that he wasn't going to sign after all. He might not have, if it hadn't been for you." Bella's voice quavered as she watched Harry anxiously, looking for some sign of softening in his countenance, but, if possible, his face grew even more grim.

Watching Bella chatter, hearing the quaver in her voice as she babbled, Curzon knew that she had spoken the truth. She was frightened. Her only thought was to postpone their joining. *It wanted only this. The one bright spot was that she was eager for me, or so I thought.* He sighed. It was as well. Perhaps another time he would feel more in control, less likely to fall on his innocent bride like a ravening beast.

He held up his hand to halt the flow of her words. "If we are not to make love tonight, I don't think sitting here next to one another is a good idea, Bella. You know when I am close to you, I tend to lose control."

"Oh, I hope so!" Relief smoothed Isabella's brow. She knuckled away her tears. "I've been so worried that you wouldn't want me." She closed the difference between them and slid her hands up his chest to grip the lapels of his robe.

"*That's* what you were afraid of?" Curzon's spirits began to lift.

"Terrified. You've known so many women, and I am so ignorant. I'm so afraid I won't measure up."

"Don't be ridiculous. I told you there has been no one for me since the day I kissed you in my studio. And I promise you there never will be. My rakish days are over."

"Then why didn't you come to my room, Harry?" She cocked her head curiously. "Why *are* you nervous?"

Curzon tugged his ear again distractedly. "I am afraid I will hurt you. You're so small, and I'm so . . ."

"You certainly are!" Mischief lit her eyes. She was suddenly the Bella he knew, and not a frightened young innocent. She tugged on his lapels, trying to get him to lower his head for a kiss.

"Don't, Bella. I won't answer for myself if you kiss me. We must approach this calmly, rationally."

He tried to put her aside, but she slipped up on his lap and managed, barely, to bestow a kiss on his lips in spite of his reluctance.

He put his arms around her then, lifting her up so that their mouths could merge in a mind-drugging kiss. Harrison was shaking when he lifted his head. "Ah, Bella. That does it! No discussion of perspective for *you* tonight!" In one motion he looped his arm under her knees and stood. Looking deeply into her eyes, he carried her to his bed. He shed his robe while she scrambled under the covers and held her arms out invitingly.

Instead of joining her immediately, he sat on the side of the bed, looking at her hungrily. "Do you know what to expect, Bella? Did your mother tell you what happens . . . ?" Somehow he couldn't imagine the ineffectual Seraphina Eardley giving her daughter a clear understanding of what her wedding night would entail.

"Mother? Silly man. Mother dissolved in a puddle when she made the attempt. But I am country-bred, Harrison. You surely don't imagine I learned nothing to the purpose on a country estate. After all, my father could talk of little else but breeding his pigs."

Curzon's shoulders shook with laughter. "It isn't exactly the same, Bella." He leaned forward, one arm on either side of her head. *Her eyes are enormous, her pupils dark. With desire?* He felt a wave of heat sweep through him at the knowledge that Bella wanted him as much as he wanted her.

"I know. The position is different. And it hurts a little the first time. But not much more than a hard pinch."

"If your mother hasn't told you this, how do you know, little Miss Innocent?"

"Grandmama told me."

Harry chuckled. "Of course. I might have known she would do it. No shrinking from her duty, that one."

He looked away for a minute. His anxieties were returning. How could he make sure that Bella's optimism was justified? It might in fact be very painful for her. A man of his size might comfortably be the lover of a tiny woman, if he had himself well under command. Otherwise . . . *For once in your life, Harrison Curzon, you will exercise iron self-control!*

"I will hurt you no more than absolutely necessary, my love, but you must do as I tell you. Lie very still . . ."

"And think about something pleasant. I know, she told me. I was surprised, for I thought making love to you *would* be pleasant." There was a lascivious gleam in her eyes. She could feel the heat of her husband's body and smell his unique masculine scent. She yearned for him to touch her, to make her his.

Harrison grinned appreciatively. "I have every intention of making it pleasant for you on future occasions. But this first time, I think the best course is to get it over with as quickly as possible."

Already the nearness of her, her light rose perfume and her own feminine scent, were beginning to work strong magic upon his body. He would have to proceed in a manner calculated to dampen his enthusiasm. *If Bella just lies there, doesn't kiss me or otherwise arouse me, I think I can manage to keep myself in hand*, he thought desperately.

He would never know if it had been a good plan, though, because when he gently pushed up Bella's nightrail just enough to do his duty, she grasped the hem and skimmed it over her head, baring his cherished little pocket-Venus to his eyes. He moaned. Unable to resist, he ran eager hands over her from shoulder to thigh. "Ah, Bella, you are as perfect as I knew you would be."

Shimmers of heat raced through Bella at his touch. She wriggled sensuously and began tugging at his nightshirt.

"No, Bella, I don't think . . ."

She sat up and slipped her hands under the shirt. "I want to see you. To touch you." She suited action to words, exploring his frame with eager hands.

Desire exploded in him, and suddenly he was touching her everywhere, just as he wanted to do, needed to do. He let her pull the nightshirt over his head and then clutched her to him. He kissed her deeply, and she moaned and kissed him back. It was too late for caution.

Bella's ardor matched his. His intimate caresses delighted her, and she urged him to join their bodies. But in spite of her eagerness, she flinched when he breached her maidenhead. Harry forced himself to be still. He lifted himself away from her, alarmed to discover he had put almost his full weight upon her. She protested, pulling him back and kissing her way from his ear, to his jawline, to his mouth. "Oh, Harry. Closer. I like the feel of you against me, surrounding me."

He gave up the struggle to be the considerate bridegroom then, and gave himself over to vigorous lovemaking that took them both to glory.

Afterward, she lay in his arms, breathing deeply and saying nothing. As he slowly recovered awareness, he felt shame at his loss of control. "Bella, love, did I hurt you? Speak to me."

She snuggled her head into the curve of his neck and began kissing him, her little tongue darting out to taste him. "Oh, Harry. I think I enjoy making love even more than painting."

A great sense of freedom filled him. His dainty young wife was a woman who was as passionate, as abandoned, as he was. And she was his, to cherish for his whole life. "And you are every bit as talented at it, too, my love."

Epilogue

"The Allegheny Mountains are not quite so stunning as the Alps, but in their own way just as beautiful." Bella daubed white onto the waterfall depicted on her large canvas and stood back to study it intently.

Harrison Curzon was sitting under a tree nearby, watching his wife of four years paint. Her manner of painting outdoors, directly from nature, was as unique as her style. Trust Bella to be unconventional in her art as in everything else. Whether indoors or out, though, he never tired of looking at her, and never failed to want her when he did so.

"I prefer to study the female form."

Bella turned to look at her handsome husband. The sun had bleached his hair and deepened his skin to a rich gold. With his shirt open at the neck and his sleeves folded back to expose his muscular forearms, he looked devastatingly attractive. She lowered her eyelids and looked at him provocatively. "I like the male form well enough, but I've painted enough pictures of you to fill Somerset House from foyer to attics."

He chuckled. "That's good, because I'm not thinking of modeling just now."

"Oh? You want *me* to pose this time?" She smirked at him before turning back to her painting.

In spite of her provocative manner, Harrison knew better than to seduce her while she was working. He was content to watch her. The sun gleamed off her golden head. Her hair was longer now. She kept it tied back out of her way with a ribbon, but curly tendrils escaped to coil around her brow and jawline.

"Did you finish your portrait of that Seneca Indian brave?"

He started. His mind had wandered to their four-year odyssey from Italy to Brazil and then to the United States. It was odd how the years since their marriage could seem at one and the same time a mere eye blink and forever.

"Something very interesting happened, so I had to start over."

She looked up from her painting again. Harrison rarely deviated from his original plan for a canvas. "What?" *Really, he just looks too tempting. And that patch of rich green grass looks too inviting.* She began cleaning her brushes as she listened to his response.

"His little daughter came over and climbed up him as if he were a tree. He was trying so hard to stand perfectly still, as I had requested. I think he saw it as a challenge to be met. But when she managed to scale him and look in his eyes, her little hand patting at his cheek, he broke into a big grin and shot me a look of such pride! I knew I had to capture that moment."

Bella covered her paints and joined her husband under the tree. "I can't wait to see the results! You have a particular genius for painting children."

He leaned down to kiss her; the gleam in her eye told him what he wanted to know, so he bore her down onto the grass.

Afterward, he pulled her into his lap and they contemplated the scenic valley below them. "Harry?"

"Ummm?" He kissed her hair.

"I want to go home."

"Home?" He felt disoriented for a moment. To their tents at camp? To the nearby settlement, where they rented a small house to store their many canvases and supplies? To New York, where they kept a *pied-à-terre* while they traveled about, painting America's spectacular scenery and native peoples?

"Where is home, after so many years of wandering?"

"England, silly."

"England!" He put her a little ways away from him to see if she was laughing. "Stuffy little England? Where your marvelous golden tan will be seen as a disfigurement? Where you will have to wear skirts all the time, and ride sidesaddle?" He was laughing down at her, but his heart was doing a little jig, because he had often thought of England lately, often wondered how his parents were, often yearned for news of his brother, who had been planning to stand for the House of Commons when last they had a letter from him over six months ago.

"Yes, England. I want to take our paintings back. What is the use of creating a magnificent body of work if no one sees them?"

Curzon studied her face carefully. "You're serious."

"Never more so. I want to see my family, especially Grandmother. Indomitable as she is, she can't live forever. And I want our first child to be born in England."

"Our . . . Bella! Are you increasing?" Had his method, learned from the French so long ago, failed her, then? She didn't seem upset, which surprised him, considering her delight when he had told her about the use of the sponge, and her meticulous observation of this precaution for these four years.

"No! If I were, I doubt we could sail in time for our child to be born in England, and anyway, what a dreadful thought, to be crossing the ocean while increasing!" She shuddered. Bella was not a good sailor.

Harry's ice blue eyes met Bella's deeper blue ones and she could see the dawning happiness in them. "You want it, too," she crowed. "I knew it! I have been feeling for a while that you would like to start our nursery. You love to paint children so much."

He stroked her head before cupping her chin in his large hand. "There is never a lack of children to paint. Don't ask for this before you are really ready, Bella, for I won't drag children about with us."

"I know. I'm ready. Oh, Harry, it's been such fun! A lifetime of memories. But . . . I hate to tell you this, for I know how much you like to travel, but I am yearning for a more settled way of life."

"Can this be my Bella?" He looked at her doubtfully. "Has one of those Indian shaman cast a magic spell that has stolen my Bella away and put a little homebody in her place?"

"The only magic is what I find in your arms, Harrison Curzon, and I can find it anywhere, including England."

"Then England it is!" He pulled her into his arms and hugged her fiercely.